Suppose I was meant for a different life—for the concert stage maybe, for champagne and speeding taxis and the lilt of exotic languages, for adventure? How would I ever find my way from Lake Marinac to the place where I truly belonged? . . .

I must have felt the deep throbbing of the dock planks before I actually saw him.

"Hi, there, Sleeping Beauty," he said, dropping down beside me.

"Roy!" I exclaimed. "You startled me! I mean, I didn't know it was you!"

"You never know!" he said. "I'll always turn up when you least expect it. . . ."

Dear Reader,

At Silhouette we publish books with you in mind. We're pleased to announce the creation of Silhouette First Love, a new line of contemporary romances written by the finest young-adult writers as well as outstanding new authors in this field.

Silhouette First Love captures many of the same elements enjoyed by Silhouette Romance readers—love stories, happy endings and the same attention to detail and description. But First Love features young heroines and heroes in contemporary and recognizable situations.

You play an important part in our future plans for First Love. We welcome any suggestions or comments on our books and I invite you to write to us at the address below.

Karen Solem
Editor-in-Chief
Silhouette Books
P.O. Box 769
New York, N.Y. 10019

THAT
SPECIAL
SUMMER
Deborah Kent

First Love from Silhouette

Published by Silhouette Books New York

America's Publisher of Contemporary Romance

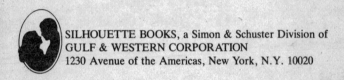 SILHOUETTE BOOKS, a Simon & Schuster Division of
GULF & WESTERN CORPORATION
1230 Avenue of the Americas, New York, N.Y. 10020

ISBN: 0-671-53322-3

First Silhouette Books printing June, 1982

10 9 8 7 6 5 4 3 2 1

THAT
SPECIAL
SUMMER

1

I'm not tall enough to reach those top shelves," Mom said, handing me the roll of shelf-lining paper. "You're much better at that sort of thing, Marcy."

It was true. Mom would have had to stand on a chair but I hardly even had to stretch up on tiptoe. I guess that's about the only real advantage I can think of to being five-eleven.

I was smoothing the paper along the third shelf when the front door banged open and Brian hollered, "Marcy? Mrs. Galaway? Anybody here?"

"In the kitchen," I called. "Where've you been all day?"

By then Mom and I had put in a good morning's work. We'd swept down the cobwebs, shaken out the rugs, scrubbed the kitchen and turned a nest of mice out of a drawer in the master bedroom. The Mac-Donald cottage was starting to look almost respectable.

"Anything I can do to help?" Brian asked with his lopsided grin.

Mom leaned her mop against the wall. "Actually we were just about to take a break," she told him. "I brought some sandwiches so we wouldn't have to run all the way home, if you'd like to join us."

Brian's grin broadened. "Trust me to show up in time for food," he said. "It must be intuition."

Dad had turned the electricity on last night, right after Mr. MacDonald called to explain that they wouldn't be coming up this summer but that they'd rented their cottage to some very nice people named Lowell from the city. He knew it was short notice, he said, but they'd be arriving to-morrow night, and maybe Mom and Dad could just straighten the place up a little. . . .

"Get out the elbow grease," Dad had said when he hung up the phone. He sighed. "I can just picture these nice people from the city—the kind that want all the fun of Lake Marinac and all the comforts of home at the same time."

Anyway, the electricity was on and Mom got some sandwiches and grapes and a big jar of apple juice out of the refrigerator. We moved the hammer, a box of nails and a can of Ajax off the kitchen table and sat down to lunch.

Brian filled our paper cups with apple juice. He had that funny, half-mischievous look that meant he was thinking of something, so I wasn't really startled when he asked, "If winter here were a musical instrument, what do you think it would be?"

I thought. Winter—so still and cold, the bare trees, the clean untracked fields of snow—winter was crossing the frozen lake, and the way your voice carried so far on a cold windless day, winter was—"A French horn," I cried, "playing very low, all by itself."

"Hey, that's good," Brian said. "I was thinking more of a guitar—the kind of piece you play, Marcy, sort of clear and soft. But yours is really even better."

We called it the impressions game. We'd been playing it since we first got to be friends back in the fourth grade. As we waited for the bus to take us down the hill to school in Callonville, Brian would say, "What kind of bird does Miss Rhodes remind you of?" or "What kind of dog was George Washington like?" So by now we could describe almost anything in terms of something else.

"How about summer?" I asked. "What kind of music?"

"Loud rock, what else?" Brian said.

"That one was too easy," I said. After all,

what other music could mean the blaze of color and noise and activity that was beginning to erupt again, as it did every summer here at Lake Marinac?

"You kids are too much." Mom laughed. "Nothing like having a couple of poets around."

"If you ask me," Brian remarked, "I prefer the French horn. Every year we go through the same thing—all these strangers coming up here, taking the place over."

"Well, we've survived it every summer," Mom said. "I guess we'll survive it again this year."

"Don't forget, if it weren't for the summer people we couldn't live here at all," I pointed out. Dad worked as official caretaker at Lake Marinac. During the winter he looked after the empty cottages to make sure pipes didn't freeze and skunks didn't hibernate under sofas. And from the end of June until Labor Day, besides listening to complaints and fixing whatever got broken, he ran Lake Marinac's only general store.

"You're right," Mom said. "We really can't complain. We practically get a vacation all winter."

But Brian could complain, and he was just about to start again when I heard the car. After the quiet of the winter, cars were still something of a novelty, and as the sound swelled I wondered who could be passing along Lakefront Road at noon on a Wednesday. I waited for the motor to purr away into the distance, but instead gravel crunched under tires and the car panted to a halt right in front of the MacDonald house.

A car door slammed and a woman's voice called, "Leave it for now, Roy. We'll bring them in later."

"I might as well carry in something, Mom," a boy's voice answered. "Give me the key to the trunk."

Around the kitchen table Mom, Brian and I exchanged startled glances. "Not the Lowells," Mom muttered. "It couldn't be—they said not till tonight. . . ."

But feet clattered on the wooden front steps and the woman's voice exclaimed, "It's not even locked! Is somebody here?"

Now the steps crossed the screened-in front porch, headed toward us through the living room. Mom shoved back her chair and scrambled to her feet. She nearly collided with the woman in the kitchen doorway, as she tried to explain, "Hi, I'm Martha Galaway. We were just here to do a little cleaning up—my daughter, Marcy, her friend Brian Townsend—you're Mrs. Lowell, aren't you?"

By now Brian and I were on our feet too. The kitchen seemed suddenly too tiny for the four of us. I followed Mrs. Lowell's gaze to the table, littered with waxed paper and grape stems. "Yes," she said ironically, "I can see you were cleaning up."

I grabbed the trash and stuffed it into the

wastebasket. All of a sudden I was seeing myself as I must look to Mrs. Lowell—a gangling giraffe of a girl, brown hair pulled straight back with a rubber band, wearing an old work shirt and cut-off jeans, dirty bare toes sticking out of worn sandals.

Beside Mrs. Lowell, we all looked hopelessly grubby. Her makeup, her tapered polished fingernails, the silvery hair in a soft coil around her head were all perfect, and her neatly pressed flowered skirt gave no hint that she'd been sitting in a hot car for the past three hours. "We're a bit early," she said, her voice cool and precise. "If it's going to be a problem . . ."

"Oh, no," Mom assured her. "And don't worry, my husband will fix that broken shade over there, and he can replace that cracked window pane and . . ."

But I didn't hear the rest of Mom's speech about repairs. There was a clatter on the porch and a boy staggered in with a suitcase in each hand. He thumped them down in the living room and hurried to join us in the kitchen. He must be Roy, I thought, and in that first instant I realized that he had a lot in common with his mother. He looked perfect, too.

He had broad shoulders that tapered to narrow hips, the sort of lithe, flowing form sculptors like to work with. And anything I say about his face will sound too good to be real—firm jaw, high cheekbones, smiling blue eyes all crowned by a mass of blond curls. But best of all, he must have been at least six-three. Roy Lowell was tall. He was taller than I was.

Boys who looked like that knew it all too well, I reminded myself. Roy was probably used to being admired and sought after. He'd expect every girl at Lake Marinac to worship at his feet all summer.

But if I felt grubby and unkempt beside Mrs. Lowell, Roy made me feel like a country hick dressed in rejects from the Goodwill box.

I just stood there mutely while we went the round of greetings. Roy nodded and smiled at Mom and Brian, but when it was my turn he repeated, "Marcy," as though he wanted to fix my name in his memory.

"Yeah, I'm Marcy," I said. Boy, did that sound dumb! I tried to think of something else to say, so he'd forget how dumb that first comment had been, but I couldn't think of anything. Roy turned away and wandered off to explore.

By now Mom had run out of things to promise and she and Mrs. Lowell eyed each other uncertainly. "My husband will be coming up on the weekends," Mrs. Lowell said. "He'll want to discuss a few things with you, I'm sure, little things the Mac-Donalds want seen to."

"Yes, of course," Mom said. Whatever they said, whatever they wanted, you always had to agree with summer people. "We'll see that everything's taken care of."

It was time for us to go. Mom gathered up the last of the grapes and the remains of the apple juice. I took the mop and the pail, and we all edged toward the back door.

Suddenly Roy called from the living room. "Hey, Mom, look. The view from here is fantastic." We turned to watch as Mrs. Lowell went to stand beside Roy at the window. They gazed out across the road to Lake Marinac, which stretched clear and shining all the way to the wooded hills down at the North Shore.

"Oh, it's beautiful," she cried, and somehow the tension that had hung between us since she entered the house broke and melted away. "Oh, just wait till Kate and your father see this, they'll love it."

When she turned back to us again, she was smiling for the first time. "This is a lovely place," she said. "It's just what I need this summer."

"I hope you'll be happy here," Mom said, and she smiled back. "Now, we better let you get settled. You have our phone number in case there's anything you need."

Mom and Brian were out ahead of me and my hand was on the doorknob when Roy said, "'Bye, Marcy. I'll see you around."

"'Bye," I said, and the way my heart skipped was really ridiculous.

"Well, they might not be too bad after all," Mom admitted once we got out of earshot. "At first I thought she'd be kind of difficult, but I guess we just kind of took her by surprise."

"You don't really have to knock yourselves out for these people you know," Brian pointed out. "They're not royalty or anything."

"They wouldn't agree with that," I said.

"Oh, come on, Marcy, don't exaggerate," Mom said quickly. "It isn't that bad."

"That guy Roy," Brian said. "He'll fit right in with Bob Hansen and that crowd from last summer. Remember them?"

I remembered them all right. They sped up and down the lake in their noisy outboard motorboats and the boys were always showing off with crazy stunts on water skis. One night someone called the police to break up a wild party they were having on the beach.

Last summer Brian and I had agreed that they were loud and obnoxious, and snobbish besides. But now, for some reason, I wondered about them. Through most of the long year, life at Lake Marinac was dull and predictable. But when the summer people arrived, they brought a hint of the city's excitement along with them. It might be fun, after all, to ride in one of those fast boats, to dance until three in the morning at one of those beach parties.

But summer kids had a lot of money to spend. They traveled to exotic places and went to fancy private schools. They were never interested in getting to know year-rounders like Brian and me.

"Well, I'm ready for a swim," Brian announced. "How about you, Marcy?"

"You read my mind," I said. "That's just what I need."

"You know," Brian said after a moment, "if that Roy were a bird he'd be a blue jay—nice to look at, but always making a racket."

But somehow I wasn't in the mood for the game anymore. "I'll meet you at our dock in ten minutes," I said.

"Make that five," Brian said, and the race was on.

2

Every spring, as soon as it was warm enough, Brian and I would canoe all the way to the North Shore and up the stream that flowed away from the lake. Brian called it our rite of spring.

But this year, week after week of clear sunny weather had slipped by and we still hadn't found time to go. I was busy with the school newspaper and practicing the guitar every day, and Brian worked weekends at the burger place down the hill. He'd be working full time all summer, too, starting Monday morning. So we had to go today.

"This could be our last chance," Brian announced when he appeared at our door after Sunday breakfast. "Even though it'll practically be a rite of midsummer by now."

All winter long we'd been able to walk

right down the middle of the road, but now we had to keep stepping aside to let cars pass. I felt almost festive as we trotted along, each swinging one of the canoe paddles. By the Fourth of July the place would really be bustling. Already cottages that had stood locked and silent since last September were bright with waving curtains, and many of the screened porches had sprouted wicker chairs, water skis and inflatable rubber rafts. The Murphy twins were back; I called hello as they sped by on their bikes licking dripping ice-cream cones. Mrs. Hansen, whose husband was the famous Dr. Hansen of New York Hospital, waved to us as she opened the car to carry in another load of suitcases.

Summer had come at last. I felt as though I had lived in an enchanted palace all winter long, a palace of snow and ice and stillness. But now the enchantment had lifted at last, the ice was gone, and the palace teemed with life.

As we passed the Lowells' cottage I saw Mrs. Lowell on the front porch looking out over the lake. I waved a greeting and she called, "You haven't seen my son, Roy, have you?"

"No," Brian called back, and I had the feeling he would have liked to add, "Thank goodness."

"He was putting the boat in the water this morning," Mrs. Lowell said. "If you run into him, tell him he's got a couple phone messages here."

"Sure, we'll tell him," I said. And I kept a lookout for someone very tall and blond as we walked along the beach.

Nearly every family at Lake Marinac had its own dock, and by now Dad had helped put them all in for the summer. So the shoreline was broken into little segments by long fingers of planking that stretched out over the water. Here and there an outboard motorboat bobbed at its moorings, and out toward the middle of the lake three sailboats skimmed the water like giant seabirds.

Brian and I walked along the beach, already dotted with sunbathers. Two little girls screamed with delight as they zoomed down the slide and tumbled into the sand.

Beyond the beach we turned onto a rock-strewn path along the water's edge, and in a few more minutes we had left the summer village behind. Off to our right rose the woods, rich with the scent of honeysuckle and ringing with birdsong.

Brian paused and pointed up a narrow trail that wound away through the underbrush. "One day this summer we've got to climb up there to the lookout," he said. "Like we did last year, remember?"

I nodded. We'd both be busy this summer, but somehow we would find the time.

Most of the summer people only glimpsed

this part of Lake Marinac as they roared past in their boats or anchored a few yards offshore to fish for the trout they stocked each spring. But Brian's family, the Townsends, lived in those woods in a little house they'd built themselves from the basement up. They liked to call themselves "twentieth-century pioneers."

The Townsends would have been an unusual family no matter where they lived. But in a place as small as Lake Marinac they were considered truly eccentric. Brian's father was a writer and he preferred the peace and quiet of their isolated life. Brian and his older brother, Tom, had grown up knowing everything about the woods: the names of birds and flowers, which wild mushrooms you could eat and which ones were poisonous, and where you could sit and wait to see a deer early in the morning. And most of the things Brian learned he tried to pass on to me.

The Townsends kept the canoe in a sandy little cove, and it lay waiting for us belly up in the morning sun. Grabbing the gunwale, we lifted together until it rolled right side up. Brian pushed and I pulled, splashing in my rubber thong sandals out into the tingling cold water until the boat broke free of the grating sand and pebbles, to float gracefully on the little ripples at the shore.

We scrambled in and took our accustomed places. I sat in the bow with the short paddle, and Brian worked his long steering paddle in the stern. In only a moment he had swung us around and we glided out of the cove into the clear open water.

We didn't talk much as we cut through the water with that easy teamwork we'd developed after canoeing together summer after summer. Once Brian said, "Hey, look up there," and we drifted for a few moments gazing at a big broad-winged hawk that hung on the air high above us.

Then I twisted around on my seat to look back at Brian. There was something almost lopsided about his face, I decided—the way his ears stuck out a little, and that cowlick on his right temple where the hair never would lie smooth. And probably no one else would even notice it now, but I could still spot the little white scar over his left eyebrow from the time he fell out of our tree house when we were ten. We saw each other almost every day, but I hardly ever really looked at him.

Because Lake Marinac was so small, with only seven families living there year round, I hadn't had much chance to make friends with kids my own age. Kathy van Horn was my best girlfriend, even though she was two years behind me in school. And Brian and I had been close ever since fourth grade. If only I could feel as relaxed and natural around other boys as I did when I was with him.

This was going to be a lonely summer, I

thought wistfully. Kathy was away visiting her cousins in Maine and Brian would be busy working most of the time. There wouldn't be much for me to do besides helping Dad out at the store, practicing the guitar and swimming off our dock by myself. By August I'd probably be looking forward to school again.

It was almost two miles to the mouth of the stream. We were nearly there when suddenly Brian paused to listen, gleaming drops of water cascading from the upraised blade of his paddle. I caught it too, then, the distant purr of an outboard motor.

"We are not alone," Brian said. He gave a sharp thrust with his paddle and the canoe leaped forward.

The purr swelled to a steady drone, and what had been only a moving dot grew magically into an orange-and-white aluminum boat that bounced toward us over the water. As it roared nearer, I recognized the tall blond boy who sat in the stern. He half-rose and waved to us, but I couldn't catch his words over the noise of the motor.

"Hi," I yelled, waving back. "Your mother said to tell you . . ."

A few yards away from us Roy cut the engine. "What?"

"Your mother said to tell you you've got a couple phone messages back at the house."

"Already? Wow, that's fantastic! Hey, I'm testing out my motor—how do you like this for power?"

He gunned the motor again and raced in a tight circle around us, churning up the water so our canoe pitched and rolled wildly. He zoomed so close I held my breath, sure he was going to ram right into us. But at the last second he waved good-bye and veered away toward the South Shore and the village.

"What did I tell you?" Brian stormed. "I told you he'd fit right in with that crowd from last summer, didn't I?"

But I didn't see why Brian should be so annoyed. Roy had just livened up the morning. The canoe still rocked on the swells that played around us. "What was he doing, anyway?" I asked finally. "I don't get it."

"Didn't you figure that out?" Brian demanded. "That whole show was for your benefit."

"Oh, come on." I felt a hot flush creep up my neck and into my cheeks. "What makes you think that?"

"I'm a guy—I ought to know." Brian let the steering paddle trail through the water. "He just got here and he's out looking to meet some girls."

He might be out looking to meet girls, I thought, but would he really bother to show off for a year-rounder like me, who'd only been to New York City once in my life, who was a sixteen-year-old giraffe on top of everything else?

I knew that being tall shouldn't bother me. But junior high had been a real nightmare. Week by week the boys tilted their heads farther back to look up at me, and they started calling me names like Beanstalk and Giganza.

I was afraid I'd never stop growing, but finally I did, of course. By now Brian was only an inch shorter than I was, and some of the boys at school had even passed me by. But I still envied all those dainty petite girls who always managed to look so sweet and feminine. I still had the nagging feeling that I was just too big to be pretty.

Not that the boys down at Callonville Regional ignored me. Now and then Peter Jaworski asked me to the movies, and sometimes Dan Holloway called me up just to talk. And Brian was as good a friend as he had ever been. But I wasn't the sort of girl they'd ever want to get serious about. To them I was probably just one of the boys.

So why should I imagine that I could ever be anything more to someone like Roy Lowell?

"Well, we made it," Brian declared, maneuvering the canoe into the mouth of the stream. "Better late than never, if you'll pardon the cliché."

"Remember last spring we saw that family of muskrats," I said. "By now those babies probably have babies."

I ducked as a thick leafy branch clutched at my hair. The canoe swished through a field of lily pads and once I saw the slim shadow of a pickerel vanish beneath the boat. For a while there was no sound but the splash of our paddles and the chorus of unseen birds.

"Brian," I began, but I caught myself just before the question escaped.

"What?" he asked.

"Oh, nothing," I said quickly. Because I had wanted to ask him to tell me again that Roy Lowell was showing off for me. And no matter how many games with words we shared, how many journeys up the stream, there were certain things I knew Brian would never understand.

3

I was pouring the nails in a long jingling river into the bin when the screen door banged and Mrs. Hansen burst into the store. Her hair was usually pretty wild and frizzy, but now it was practically standing on end. "Where's your father, Marcy?" she demanded, her voice shaking. "We've got an awful problem at the house."

Dad emerged from the back room, wiping his hands on his overalls. He took in the situation at a glance and put on his efficient business-as-usual voice as he asked, "What seems to be the trouble?"

"There's a *bat!*" Mrs. Hansen jabbered. "I was watering my African violets and the thing came swooping out from under the shade—scared ten years off my life."

"Did you open the window?" Dad asked. "It'd probably fly right out by itself."

"I wasn't about to stick around there doing anything," Mrs. Hansen said. "I ran straight over here to get you."

"Okay then." Dad sighed and turned to me. "You hold the fort, Marcy. I shouldn't be too long."

"I can't stand them—horrible, creepy things—and they get tangled up in your hair you know. . . ." Mrs. Hansen's voice trailed away up the road. How could people be so lost and helpless, I wondered. People like my folks and Brian's family just took these things as part of life, but to the summer people anything that went amiss was a calamity.

So there I was, left minding the store on a beautiful Saturday morning. I knew that once the bat was taken care of, Mrs. Hansen would think of ten or eleven more things for Dad to do and he wouldn't be back till lunchtime. I could be out on our dock, reading and lapping up the sun, diving into the delicious cool of the lake whenever I got too hot. But instead I was stuck behind the counter in the empty store.

Business was slow for a while. Mrs. Abano came in for a quart of skimmed milk, and Mr. Douglas, a year-rounder from over on Old Lane, bought a pair of shears. The Murphy twins, Peter and Paul, came in to finger everything and finally selected two comic books apiece.

I was just ringing up their purchase when the screen door banged again, and

Roy Lowell strode in. He tossed me a smile and went over to the magazine rack.

"Oh, hey, I want one of those," said one of the twins, the one with the big wad of bubble gum in his mouth. He darted away from the counter and came back with a package of chocolate cupcakes.

"I'm gonna tell," his brother taunted. "Mom said no snacks."

"Oh, yeah?" the first twin shot back. "If you tell, then I'll tell how it was you that broke the hammock."

"You better not, or else . . ."

I think the twin with the gum struck the first blow. But in the next ten seconds it was impossible to tell who was hitting whom. Somebody was howling, "No fair! No fair!" and the comic books scattered onto the floor. Two identical faces grew red with rage.

"Hey, hey, cool it, you guys," cried Roy, but he was grinning and I guess the twins knew he was really enjoying the scene. I was the one who had to pry the two of them apart, sort out their purchases and send them on their way with a warning about never coming in again if they couldn't learn to behave themselves.

At last they were gone. I sank down onto a stool and brushed some stray hair out of my eyes.

"Phew!" Roy exclaimed. "I thought there was going to be blood and gore in here any minute. Is running the store always this hazardous?"

"No," I said. "Most of the time it's really kind of boring. At least they livened things up a little."

Roy leaned on the counter. "Can you tell which is which? They look as though they were cloned."

"I don't even try." I liked having Roy in the store. Suddenly I didn't mind being shut in all morning anymore. I tried to think of something bright and witty to say, something that would make him want to stay and talk for a while. But I couldn't think of anything. "Were you looking for something?" I asked finally. "Can I help you?"

"No, not really. I just thought I'd come in and look around, and help you pass the time a little, Marci-oh."

"Oh, thanks." I felt confused all of a sudden. I didn't quite know what to do with my hands; they started playing with a pad and pencil that lay next to the cash register.

"Do you work here regular hours or what?" Roy asked.

"It's hard to say. I just sort of fill in when they need me."

"This is the busy season for you guys— with all of us coming up for the summer."

"Oh, we keep busy all right." For some reason the picture of Mrs. Hansen popped into my head, and I giggled.

"What's so funny?" Roy wanted to know.

So I told him about Mrs. Hansen and the bat. "She was afraid it'd get tangled up in her hair," I said. "And I just started thinking—her hair's always all fluffed up on top of her head, there could be two or three bats in there all the time, and how could anybody ever tell?"

We both started to laugh then. It was easier to talk to Roy than I had ever expected.

"Hey," Roy said all of a sudden, "you want to go water-skiing this afternoon?"

He caught me so completely by surprise that for a second or two I just stared at him. Before I could think clearly again, he asked anxiously, "You do water-ski, don't you? I mean you know how?"

"Oh, sure," I said with a vigorous nod. "I haven't been out yet this summer, but—"

"Well, come with us, then," Roy said. "Me and a couple of other kids are going around two-thirty."

I hesitated. I had nothing in common with Roy and a bunch of other summer kids. I'd feel hopelessly backward around them. I'd never find anything to say. . . .

"You really ought to come," Roy said. "You can't just work all the time, you know."

There was something about his smile and the brightness of his voice that I couldn't resist. "Okay," I said. "I can't argue with you. I'll come."

"Good show," Roy said. He wandered

over to the magazine rack and leafed through the new *Isaac Asimov* magazine.

I could guess what Brian would say if he knew I was going water-skiing with Roy. But Roy was friendly and fun to be with. There was no reason why Brian should object to him.

The trouble with Brian, I decided, was that he was too narrow-minded. The Townsends had lived up in the woods for so long that they'd lost touch with the rest of the world. But just because Brian liked being a hermit, that didn't mean I had to isolate myself too.

No, I thought as Roy spun the rack of postcards, I wasn't meant to be a recluse. Maybe this summer would be a turning point in my life. I was going out water-skiing with Roy this afternoon. That was certainly a good beginning.

"Guess I'll take these." Roy returned to the counter holding out a bunch of Lake Marinac postcards. "I've got to let the gang back home know where I am—make them all jealous."

There were four of them—glossy scenes of the lake at sunset, racing sailboats, and children playing on the beach. I rang them up and slipped them into a small paper bag.

"You know where our dock is?" Roy asked.

I nodded, and he went on, "See you there around two-thirty."

"See you then," I echoed, bright and

breezy, as if I always went around making appointments with guys like Roy Lowell.

Roy had almost reached the door when it swung open again. For a second I didn't recognize the slim red-haired girl who stepped inside, not until Roy exclaimed, "Hey, it's Eilene Flannery. Eilene Flannery of Sunnyside Lane."

I'd been seeing Eilene around every summer since I was eleven. I remembered how once we had worked quietly together, building an elaborate sand castle with bridges and towers and dungeons. But most of the time we'd just smiled and said hi to each other and gone our separate ways. Roy was amazing, I thought. This was only the beginning of his first summer at Lake Marinac and already he knew her better than I did.

"You want to go out water-skiing this afternoon?" Roy asked her. "A whole bunch of us are going—me and Bob Hansen and this girl he just met named Carla, and Marcy's coming, aren't you, Marcy?"

"Sure, I'm coming." I tried to keep the doubt from creeping into my voice. After all, it wasn't as if Roy had made a date with me. He had told me that other kids were going too. There was no good reason why I should feel this twinge of disappointment.

"Water-skiing!" Eilene was saying. "Wow, I haven't been in ages. You think I could forget how?"

"You can't forget how," Roy said. "It's like riding a bike."

"So who says I can ride a bike?" Eilene giggled. "I'm the original klutz. Come on, you can help me—I've got to get all this stuff for my mother."

Their voices rose and fell as they made there way back to the grocery section. I couldn't catch everything they were saying, but apparently Eilene had said something very funny about Jell-O. I couldn't imagine what could be so funny about it, but Roy swayed with laughter, and Eilene half collapsed against a shelf of canned goods, knocking three cans of dog food to the floor. That got them laughing harder than ever.

Just then Dad came through the door. Roy and Eilene glanced up guiltily and scrambled after the rolling cans. I was glad Dad was back, grateful to be distracted from the back of the store.

"Well, no more bats in the belfry." Dad chuckled. "You know where it had gotten to? I found it in the bathroom, hiding behind a towel that was hanging on the door. I shooed it right out the window, but the poor lady was a wreck."

Eilene let out another shrill giggle. I glimpsed a swift movement, as if Roy had tried to tickle her, but I couldn't be certain.

"You don't need me for anything else, do you, Dad?" I asked.

"No, you can take off if you want to. Nothing exciting while I was gone?"

"Nothing exciting."

Dad waved me toward the door. "Tell your mother I'll close up here around four."

"Sure," I said. "I'll tell her."

It didn't make any sense. Roy had just said he'd dropped in to help me pass the time a little, and he'd very generously invited me to go water-skiing, to join a group of his other friends. I hardly knew him, and it wasn't as though he'd asked me out for a date.

So why should I have this weird tightened-up feeling when I saw how he acted with Eilene? When I looked at Eilene I felt taller and gawkier than ever, and I knew I had nothing quick and funny to say. And when I thought of Roy, I longed to be different.

It was a relief to get away from the store. I hurried down the road toward home, putting their laughter farther and farther behind me.

It was one-thirty by the time I had finished helping Mom with the lunch dishes. I wasn't due at Roy's dock for an hour. That left me a piece of time big enough for practicing the guitar.

Whenever anyone at school found out I played the guitar, they thought right away that I played rock or country music. They'd ask me which band I played with or if I ever performed for Sweet Sixteen parties. They didn't know what to say when they found out that I played classical guitar. A lot of the time they didn't even know what it was.

Sometimes I wished I could have chosen something more practical, something other kids could have shared with me. But I hadn't really had a choice. I'd been fascinated by classical guitar since I was twelve, when I heard Andrés Segovia play on television and thought there couldn't be anything more beautiful in the whole world.

I was sure I'd never find a teacher anywhere near Lake Marinac. Yet, three days before my thirteenth birthday, I spotted the ad in the *Oracle*, our local weekly. Here was a woman from Spain who had studied at the finest conservatories of music in Europe. Now, with her American husband, she had settled right down the hill in Callonville, where she offered lessons in piano and classical guitar. Her name was Carmen Calderón.

Dad had been skeptical. "You'll get tired of it in two months," he'd said. "I remember when I took tuba lessons back in high school—I never found time to practice."

But there was nothing else I wanted for my birthday, and finally Dad agreed to let me try a few lessons, just to see how I'd do. Now I'd been studying for three years. Miss Calderón was a stern teacher, and sometimes she brought me close to tears of frustration. But she made me work hard and slowly I was learning my way around in that wilderness among the strings.

I glanced over the opening measures of my new piece, a waltz by Fernando Sor, and stretched my left hand into position for the first chord. The strings quivered at the slightest touch, sprinkling the room with delicate silver notes. But yesterday the piece had gone much better. This afternoon I limped through the first bars, stumbled over what should have been a graceful turn, and jolted to a halt at the bridge that led to the second section.

I went back to the beginning and tried to get a good running start, but it was no use. My fingers kept tangling up and deadening the strings. I just couldn't concentrate.

I sighed and laid the guitar on my bed. I stared down at my hands. My nails were chipped and dirty from digging in the garden, and there was a big ugly scrape on my right shin from when I climbed over the fence to pick some lilies yesterday morning. I looked like an overgrown tomboy, I thought in disgust. If I had any intention of spending the afternoon with Roy and Eilene and the rest of their friends, I'd have to do something about myself in a hurry.

I took a quick shower, cleaned and filed my nails, and braided my hair and wound it around my head in a way I hoped would hold up even when it got wet. By the time I set out in my thong sandals and my yellow two-piece bathing suit I felt almost present-able. But even if I looked my best, what would I ever find to say?

When I arrived, there was already a gang out at the end of the Lowells' dock. Roy was helping Eilene into the orange-and-white outboard, while a slender brown-haired girl stood quietly waiting her turn. Maybe it was an accident, but when the boat dipped and Eilene nearly lost her balance, she giggled and swayed against Roy's shoulder.

For a second I wanted to turn and leave before they ever saw me. But just then Roy looked up and waved to me. "Hey, Marci-oh!" he called to me. "You finally made it."

I walked slowly out along the dock, my sandals slapping against the planks.

"We're heading out to the ski raft," Roy explained. "Carla and Bob are already out there."

I stepped into the boat and took the mid-dle seat beside Eilene, who was so busy watching Roy that she hardly seemed to notice me. But the brown-haired girl, who was settled in the bow by this time, gave me a friendly smile. "Hi, I'm Liz," she said. "Don't you live up here year round?"

"Yeah," I said. It had to come out sooner or later, but I hadn't thought they would hit me with it the very first thing.

But to my surprise Liz leaned forward with interest. "Hey, I bet it's neat up here in the winter," she said. "It must be beautiful with the snow and everything."

"It is," I said. "A couple months ago you could walk right across the lake."

Before I could say more, Roy clambered into the stern and the motor coughed into life. "Five, four, three, two, one—blast off!" he cried, and we roared away from the dock, churning up a wake of foam and spray.

No one tried to talk much above the roar of the motor, and in only a minute or two we reached the green ski raft. It bobbed at anchor only a few hundred yards from shore, a series of broad planks nailed to half a dozen floating barrels. Bob Hansen stood up to greet us—burly and broad-shouldered, he looked like he'd be more at home in a helmet and a padded football uniform. I decided the plump blonde lying on a pink beach towel had to be Carla.

"Okay, everybody ready?" Bob asked when Roy cut the motor. "Who's going first?"

"We'll cast lots," Roy said. He nudged the barrel with the side of the boat and Carla squealed as the raft lurched.

"I know, I know!" Eilene exclaimed. "We'll have a raffle. We do it all the time at Hawkins to see who gets seconds on dessert."

"What do you mean, a raffle?" Roy asked.

Eilene twisted around on the seat to face him. "Okay, let's see if I can explain it. First you pick a number from one to five."

"Two," Roy said promptly.

"No, no, you aren't supposed to *tell* anybody," Eilene cried. "You just think it to yourself, and then when I say 'shoot' you hold up that many fingers. . . ."

"How many?" Bob asked.

"That many!" Eilene was getting an attack of the giggles. "The number you thought. You hold up that many fingers."

"I do?" Roy asked. For some reason he seemed to think it was all very funny too. "Just me, all by myself?"

"No!" Eilene shrieked. "Everybody holds them up, whatever number they thought of. Not just you."

"Yeah, not just you," Bob repeated. He was getting swept along by Eilene's giggles too. "What makes you think you're so special, Lowell?"

"Hey, come on, this is serious," Eilene protested, breaking into another spasm of laughter. "We do it all the time at my school."

Maybe something was wrong with me, but I just didn't think it was very funny. I glanced over at Carla—she smiled drowsily as she rummaged in her straw beach bag and it was hard to tell what she thought. But when I looked at Liz, she seemed to sense my bewilderment. She rolled her eyes and tapped her forehead as though she thought they'd all gone around the bend.

"I've got a better idea," Roy said when they calmed down a little. "It's perfectly chauvinistic—ladies first. I'll take Liz first, then Carla, Marcy and Eilene, last but not least."

Eilene opened her mouth to argue, but Roy winked at her and she merely giggled again and said, "Oh, you always win."

"And somebody better ride along with me," Roy went on, "to keep an eye on whoever's skiing while I drive."

"Not me," Eilene declared. "I'm gonna lie up there on the raft and catch some rays till my turn comes up."

"I'll go," Bob volunteered. "You girls can have the raft to yourselves with your sun cream and your gossip and everything."

It took some complicated maneuvering, but Eilene and I scrambled up onto the raft, Bob lowered himself into the boat, and Liz splashed in over the side and swam around to the stern to grab the skis Roy handed her.

The raft was anchored at the edge of a sandbar, so the water came only to Liz's shoulders. She managed to work her feet into the rubber shoes on the skis, balancing on one leg and then the other. Roy threw her the rope and she clutched the handle as though it were a lifeline.

"Keep your skis straight," Roy told her. "Look out you don't let the tips cross." He moved the boat ahead a few yards and the rope drew taut until Liz was crouching on the skis with the tips jutting out of the water.

"Ready?" Roy shouted.

"I guess so," Liz said, but she looked a little scared.

"Okay, here goes," called Roy. The boat leaped forward, and the rope pulled Liz to her feet. For an instant I saw a grin flash across her face. Then she was gliding away across the lake.

As the roar of the motor faded into the distance, I felt suddenly abandoned. Roy had invited me, and Liz had been friendly, but here I was alone on the ski float with Eilene and Carla, and I hardly knew either one of them. If we just watched Liz, maybe we wouldn't have to have a conversation— but as Liz grew smaller and smaller far down the lake, Eilene turned to Carla and asked, "You didn't come up here last summer, did you?"

Carla stretched out her legs in the sun and unwrapped a candy bar. "No," she said. "My dad's company sent him to Italy. We were in Venice for six months."

"Oh, Venice!" Eilene made a face as if she smelled something rotten. "When you read about it, it's supposed to be such a beautiful city. But really it's just damp and dirty and falling apart."

"Oh, I guess it wasn't so bad once I got used to that mildewy smell all the time," Carla said. "The Italian guys made up for it."

"Yuck! I couldn't *stand* those Italian

guys!" Eilene exclaimed. "They're not suave at all—not like the French. Did you get to Paris?"

"We got a month travel time before we came home," Carla said. "So we went to Paris and Spain—"

"Spain!" I cried. "You've been to Spain?" They both turned and looked at me in surprise. "Yeah," Carla said. "Have you?"

"No," I said. "But I've always wanted—I mean, from everything I've ever read about it, I bet it's really interesting."

"It's okay," Carla said. "But you ought to go to Italy or France, that's the real Europe." The last of the candy bar disappeared. She crumpled the wrapper and I winced as she tossed it into the lake.

"When we were over there," Eilene added, "my father said you could tell the Spaniards haven't created anything new since the Armada was defeated."

They've created wonderful music, I wanted to protest. What about Andrés Segovia and Joaquín Rodrigo, and even Carmen Calderón? How could they be so nonchalant, so bored, talking about Europe? If I could have spent six months in Venice . . . But I could hardly imagine such a thing.

In a few more minutes the boat swung back toward the raft. Liz climbed up beside me and Carla jumped into the water to put on the skis. She was awkward and fumbling and I wondered if she had ever water-skied before.

"Roy, not so fast, not so fast," she shrieked as he speeded up the boat. She let go of the handle and thrashed around in the water, hampered by the skis still clinging to her feet.

"Relax, you're not going to drown," Roy told her. He threw her the rope again and this time she hung on and somehow got to her feet. She was wobbly, but at least she didn't fall.

"Hey, you did okay," I told Liz. "Have you skied much before?"

She tugged a comb through her wet tangled hair. "A couple of times. This was probably my best, though. I bet you've been water-skiing since you could walk, living here all the time."

"Oh, not really." For a while the three of us sat in silence, watching Carla as she glided toward the North Shore. At a distance she no longer looked awkward, but floated along with steady grace.

Eilene smoothed her beach towel and stretched out along the far edge of the float. "What school do you go to, Liz?" she asked.

"Branley. It's not as good as Hawkins, I guess, but at least they're big on music."

"Hawkins is a drag," Eilene corrected her. "I'd much rather go to a day school. At Branley at least you don't have some old bag of a housemother breathing down your neck all the time."

"No, but it's bad enough the way they pile on the homework," Liz said. "They think you've got nothing better to do. They act as if you should never have time to go out or anything."

I dangled my bare feet in the water and let their words drift around me until they became almost meaningless. I had nothing to say to them, and they had nothing to say to me. I went to plain old Callonville Regional High School, and the most exciting trip I'd ever taken had been a weekend in New York City with Mom and Dad two years ago. Liz and Carla and Eilene might tolerate my presence, but they'd never accept me into their crowd. And Roy—he was just trying to be friendly. But he couldn't possibly be interested in me, with sophisticated girls like them to choose from.

A breeze came up, and I rescued Carla's towel before it blew into the lake. Why had I gotten myself into this? Here I sat, stranded on the raft among these strangers, with no hope of escape.

Carla must have taken a fall somewhere out of sight around the point, because when the boat came back, she sat in the bow, bedraggled and forlorn. I handed her her towel as she hoisted herself up onto the raft, and she wrapped herself up like a mummy.

"You're next, Marci-oh," Roy called. "Let's see you get wet."

I stood up and glanced back at Eilene and Liz, sprawled on the planks of the raft, and Carla huddled up in her pink beach towel.

Then I sprang into the cool clear water and reached up to take the skis Roy passed over the stern.

It always gave me an odd ungainly feeling, floundering around in the water with those long pieces of wood fastened to my feet. For a moment I paddled with my hands to keep my balance. Then Roy threw me the rope and suddenly I was in position, my knees bent, my arms outstretched, my hands tingling with every twitch and tremor of the rope.

"All set," I called to Roy. The purr of the motor swelled, the rope drew taut, and in the next moment I broke clear of the water and stood erect, the wind in my face, skimming over the lake behind the roaring boat.

I saw Roy's hands clapping, and his mouth shaped words I couldn't hear. I grinned at him and yelled, "I'm flying!" knowing that he couldn't hear a word I said.

And really it was like flying. My feet barely touched the surface of the lake. I felt as though nothing was holding me up. There was only the glorious rush of wind and spray, the exhilarating speed as I raced past the beach, past the cove, past the big rock where someone had once painted the word PEPPERTOWN. . . .

I wasn't prepared for the sudden swerve that jerked me out of the boat's smooth shining wake. The choppy water nearly threw me over sideways, but I managed to keep my balance and find my way back to the wake. A few seconds later the boat veered again, even more sharply than before. But this time I was ready for it. I shifted my weight and kept myself upright while I maneuvered back into the clear track the boat cut for me through the water.

When I looked up again, Roy and Bob were applauding, and their cheers carried over the racket of the motor. Roy was purposely giving me a rough ride, I realized, teasing me, trying to see just how much I could take. I grinned back and let go of the handle with one hand to wave. No matter how hard he tried, I promised myself, he wouldn't make me fall. I might not go to a fancy private school, but I did know how to water-ski.

We approached the North Shore and the mouth of the stream where Brian and I had paddled the canoe. Roy swung the boat around back toward the raft again. He made sure it was an exciting trip all the way, slowing and speeding up when I least expected it, twisting and zigzagging back and forth across the lake. And each time I succeeded in keeping my skis parallel beneath me, he and Bob clapped and let out wild rodeo war whoops of delight.

At last the green raft bobbed before us. Roy cut the motor, the rope went slack, and I splashed into the water. In the sudden quiet Eilene, Liz and Carla were all talking at once, shouting, "Wow!" and "We can't beat that!" and "See, I thought you'd be good."

"Hey, Marci-oh," Roy called. "You said you could water-ski, but you didn't tell me you'd been in the Olympics."

I waded over to the boat and handed in the wet skis. "Hardly," I said. "It's just that I've done it a lot, that's all." My face must already be flushed from the wind, so maybe no one could tell I was blushing.

"I bet you know how to drive a boat, too," Roy said. "Hop in. You can drive me when it's my turn to ski."

He held out his hand. I grabbed it and hauled myself up over the side of the boat. For a moment I crouched in the bottom, water streaming from my wet bathing suit. Then, as I moved to sit beside Bob on the middle seat, Roy slid over and made room for me beside him in the stern.

"Okay, Eilene Flannery," Bob cried with a note of challenge in his voice, "On your mark, get set—"

"Prepare to meet your maker," Roy shouted as Eilene jumped in and swam around behind the boat. "Hope you made out your last will and testament."

But even while Eilene was putting on the skis Roy turned back to look at me, and I saw admiration shining in his face. "You ought to come skiing with us more often," he said. "We go pretty nearly every afternoon around this time."

"I'd love to," I told him. We were very

crowded, the two of us there on the narrow seat. Was it just an accident when his hand rested against mine and our knees touched?

"You're really okay, you know that?" Roy said. "I mean it."

And I felt that perhaps it didn't matter after all where I came from and where I went to school. For that precious moment, with Roy's hand on mine, I felt like the most attractive, wittiest, smartest girl in the whole world.

4

Well, that should do it," said Brian's mother, Mrs. Townsend. She swirled the last of the blueberries under the running water and emptied the colander into the bowl. "They'll be perfect for dessert."

"Anything else I can do?" I asked.

She thought for a moment, her hands already busy slicing a cucumber for the salad. "You could go start calling my husband," she said. "It'll take a good ten minutes before he listens to you."

"I better go with you, Marcy," Brian said, grinning. "When he's out there in his study he just tunes out the world."

We got up from the big round kitchen table and I followed Brian out the back door. We crossed a grassy clearing, passed the neat fenced-in vegetable garden, and

Brian pushed open the door to the shed that served as his father's study.

Mr. Townsend didn't even glance up. He bent over his paper-strewn desk, clattering away at an old Underwood typewriter. The room overflowed with books—on shelves, in boxes and just stacked up on the floor. And on two of the walls hung long bulletin boards covered with Mr. Townsend's notes to himself. From the doorway I read a couple of them: "Quality of mind—his waking dreams en route to Rivington Street" and "Why did Col. Buendía remember the ice?" Mr. Townsend said they were thoughts and ideas that helped him with his writing, but none of them ever made much sense to me.

Brian waited until his father's fingers came to a pause over the keys. "Dad," he said quietly, like someone trying to waken a sleeper without startling him. "Dad, lunch is about ready."

Then Mr. Townsend turned to us, his face unshaven, his eyes red and tired. He nodded slowly. "I'll be right there," he said, and turned away again.

But before his work could engulf him once more, Brian said more insistently, "Rainbow trout, Dad. That four-pounder that Tom caught this morning."

"Sounds good," Mr. Townsend said in a faraway voice. "Tell your mother I'll be there in five—better make it ten. . . ."

"You know what she'll say to that," Brian

said. "Come on, everything'll be getting cold."

Mr. Townsend looked at me with the hint of a mischievous grin. "My entire family," he said, "is dedicated to the proposition that I shall not be permitted to starve." But he pushed back his chair, cast a last wistful glance around his study and followed us out into the sunlight.

"What are you working on now?" I asked him as we reached the kitchen again.

"It's a new novel," Mr. Townsend said. "Stream of consciousness. Giving me the devil of a time, though. I'm trying to get the unique traits of each character's thoughts, so it's as if each one speaks with a different voice inside his mind."

"Sit down," Brian's mother urged. "Let's eat the fish while it's still hot."

We all took seats around the table, and Brian's older brother, Tom, served the fish from the steaming platter.

"I'm afraid it's kind of esoteric," Mr. Townsend went on. "But if I'm lucky, maybe one of the university presses will publish it."

The fish was delicious, "So fresh it might swim off your plate," as Tom put it. There were salad and beans and peas from the garden, and of course wild blueberries for dessert. Brian and I had filled two metal pails with them that morning, scrambling over rocks and logs, warning each other about patches of poison oak.

"Anybody for mint tea?" Mrs. Townsend asked. "It's from the garden too."

"Sure," I said. I helped clear the table and she put some water on. I'd spent so much time at the Townsends' over the past years that I moved around their kitchen as if I were in my own home.

"Marcy, you better tell your dad I killed a copperhead on the path," said Tom. Tom was twenty, and he went to the community college down in Callonville.

"Only one?" I asked. "Don't they usually run in pairs?"

"That's just it," Tom said. "We all better be on our guard for a while."

"I'll never forget the first time I saw one of them—actually there were two," Mrs. Townsend said, pouring the tea. "It was that first winter we spent here. We only had two rooms finished off enough so you could live in them then. But one morning I went out into one of the half-built rooms, what's Brian's room now, and there they were curled up under some boards in the corner, nice and cozy—hibernating, you know."

"When she didn't run back to the city after that one, I knew she'd stick it out here," Brian's father said. "That was the toughest winter we ever spent here—no electricity, the four of us cooped up in two little rooms."

"How old was I then, about six?" Brian mused. "The thing I remember most about it was how cold it was. Me and Tom would crawl under that big quilt Grandma Townsend made and Dad would read to us out of the encyclopedia. We'd take turns telling him what to look up for us."

"And that lantern," Tom added. "It made kind of a hissing, sputtering noise, and the house always smelled like kerosene."

"Back then I was still dreaming of the best-seller list," Mr. Townsend said wryly. "I kept waiting for the world to beat a path to my door."

"Fine, and what would we do with the world at our door?" Brian's mother said. "We've spent all these years holding the world at bay so you could work in peace."

Mr. Townsend grinned. "Well, I'm entitled to a little inconsistency once in a while," he said. "Every now and then I get to thinking it might be nice to write the ultimate blockbuster, have reporters making up juicy stories about us all."

"You'll despise it when it happens," Mrs. Townsend said.

Mr. Townsend had sold lots of short stories to obscure literary magazines, and he'd even published a novel called *Nutcracker Suite*. I tried to read it once, but I couldn't understand most of it and never finished the first chapter. I guess most people had the same problem, because it sold only 517 copies.

But Mrs. Townsend and Tom and Brian never complained. Mom and Dad were always trying to figure out how they managed to make ends meet, but somehow they survived. They did whatever they had to do so Mr. Townsend could go on with his work.

"How are your guitar lessons coming, Marcy?" Mrs. Townsend asked, taking me by surprise.

"I've been working on a new piece for the past ten days or so," I said. I set down my mug of tea. "It's a really hard one."

"When are you going to play it for me?" Brian wanted to know.

"Oh, it's still got a long way to go," I said. "I couldn't—"

"That's okay. It's my day off today, so I get to do what I want," Brian proclaimed. "And I want to go over to your place this afternoon and listen to your new piece."

"How about a couple of my old ones instead?"

"Don't argue with me on my day off," Brian said, and we both laughed.

Mr. Townsend rose and slipped back to his study. Tom had a paper to write for one of his summer-school courses, so he didn't stay around very long either. Brian's mother assured us that she had the dishes under control, and in another minute we were on the path heading back toward the village.

"Is your job really awful?" I asked him. I found myself walking very carefully, keeping a watchful eye open to glimpse a copperhead among the fallen leaves.

"It would be if it weren't for the crew

working there," Brian said. And he began
to tell me all about them—about Pete, who
plowed through his work like a bulldozer,
never looking right or left; and Julie, who
sang songs from Gilbert and Sullivan all
the while she was frying hamburgers; and
Dolly, who lost her class ring in a vat of cole
slaw.

At last we were off the path and crossing
the public beach. Brian had just launched
into a description of Louise, his boss, who
was having boyfriend troubles and spent
most of her time studying her horoscope,
when a familiar voice called, "Hey, Marci-
oh, whatcha up to?" and Roy loped toward
us along the sand.

"Nothing much," I said. "It's Brian's day
off, we're just wandering around."

"When are you coming water-skiing
again?" Roy asked. "You've got to give
those other girls a lesson."

Brian lagged a step or two behind, and I
glanced back at him anxiously. "I meant to
tell you," I explained, "I went water-skiing
with Roy last week—with Roy and a bunch
of other kids."

"Do you water-ski, Brian?" Roy asked.
"You ought to come with us sometime, too."

"Thanks," Brian said, but he didn't sound
very grateful.

Roy must have been a little startled—I
know I was. He turned back to me as if
Brian weren't really part of the conversa-

tion. "Come by the dock any afternoon. There's usually a gang hanging out over there."

"Okay," I said, smiling. "I'll probably do that."

When Roy was gone, I turned back to Brian. "It's a lot of fun, really. You should come next time."

"You've got to be kidding." Brian scuffed up a cloud of fine white sand. "What makes you think I'd want to do that?"

"Well, I don't see why not. And Roy just invited you."

"I doubt if he really meant it," Brian grumbled. "And even if he did . . ."

"Well, he invited me, and I know he meant it, because the last time I went he was very nice." I was starting to get mad. "And I don't see why you had to act that way toward him just now, either."

"What way?"

"You know what I'm talking about."

There were two things that always annoyed me about Brian—he'd never admit when he was wrong, and he'd never say he was sorry. We reached the far side of the beach and walked in silence along Lakefront Road. Why did Brian have to act like that just now when Roy and I were starting to get to know each other?

Neither of us spoke for a while, until Brian burst out, "I thought you had better sense, Marcy Galaway. Can't you tell Roy's just the kind of guy who likes to have a whole bunch of girls fluttering around him? But in the long run, none of those summer kids will ever accept people like you and me."

"You're not being fair," I said. "You're not giving them a chance."

"Is it true or is it not true," Brian began, "that you have been here every summer of your life and you have never yet made friends with any member of that crowd. Why do you suppose that is?"

For a second I was afraid he had me. But then an answer came to me, and it had to be the right one. "I never tried to get to know them," I said. "Somewhere—I don't know if it was from my family or what— somewhere I just got the idea that I should leave them alone. But that's really dumb. Roy is so nice, and Eilene and this girl Liz—they're interesting. They've traveled and read books and everything."

Brian shrugged. "I think the crew down at McDonald's is a lot more interesting than Roy Lowell's crowd," he said. "But you'll find out."

I shouldn't have tried to play the new piece for Brian when we got to my house. My heart just wasn't in it. Brian paced up and down as I played, his hands in his pockets, pausing now and then to glance out the window. I wasn't surprised when he said he had a lot to do and he'd have to leave early. I think I actually felt relieved when he was gone.

5

This was not how a sixteen-year-old girl was supposed to spend her summer vacation, I thought gloomily. I sat sprawled in a lounge chair on the front porch watching the people who passed by along Lakefront Road, trying to finish the lower left-hand corner of a crossword puzzle and wondering what was the matter with Brian.

It wasn't like us to argue, and when we did disagree, it was usually over in a few hours. But I hadn't heard from him since the day I had lunch at his house, and it had been nearly a week now. Naturally the Townsends had no phone, so I couldn't call him and couldn't hope that he would call me. But usually he'd drop by whenever he had a free hour or two and we'd go canoeing or take a swim or just sit and talk. Brian

was staying away on purpose, and I didn't
like it at all.

But just because Brian was keeping to
himself that shouldn't condemn me to a life
of solitude. I had met plenty of new people
this summer, and if I weren't so shy, I could
go and join them—Liz, and Carla, and
Roy. . . .

I glanced down at the newspaper again.
"Tearful mother," the definition read. It
was in five letters, beginning with N . . .

A boy sped by on a bicycle, saluting the
world with a brisk ring of his bell. Mrs.
Hansen came up the road, a beach towel
over her arm, her hair as unruly as ever.
"You going up to the corn roast tonight?"
she called to Mrs. Murphy, who was clip-
ping back her rhododendrons.

"Never miss it," Mrs. Murphy called
back. "Mother's night off."

Everyone else had destinations and
plans, but I just sat here alone on the front
porch, watching the world go by, stuck on
the lower left corner.

Well, nobody had forced me to sit here.
Only my own shyness kept me from heading over to the Lowells' dock right now—
shyness, and maybe a twinge of concern
about all of the things Brian had said.

I flung the paper aside, jumped to my feet
and raced to change into my bathing suit.
Roy had said I should come by any afternoon, so what was wrong with today?

I was amazed by how much better I felt

the moment I made the decision. For the first time I noticed what a bright breezy day it was, and how lovely the sailboats looked scudding across the lake. The Murphys' black cocker spaniel, Tania, bounded down their front steps to greet me, and I bent to stroke her long silky ears.

"Good afternoon, Marcy," called old Mr. Douglas, out for his daily walk up to the store. "How'd you folks like all that rain we had the other day?"

"It was good for the garden, I guess." I slowed my steps to walk beside him. Mr. Douglas was one of the first people ever to settle year round at Lake Marinac. He'd lived here for thirty-five years, since he retired from pitching for the Boston Red Sox. He remembered back before any of the cottages had been built, when visitors had to stay at the old hunting and fishing lodge. That place had been a tumbledown wreck when I was little, and they tore it down when I was nine to build the community house in its place.

"I've got something for your mother," Mr. Douglas said. "I was going through some old boxes and I came across a pretty blue-and-white plate. It was my wife's, you see. I don't know if it's anything so special, but she can have it if she'd like it."

"Oh, I know she'd like to see it," I said. "I'll let her know, okay?"

There were voices behind us, people overtaking us because we walked so slowly. A girl gave a shimmering laugh, and a boy said, "Come on—really? She came right out and *said* that?"

I knew who it was, but I turned just to be sure. Roy drew closer and closer with his long supple strides. His face glowed and I caught the wonder in his voice, as though he had never heard anything so fascinating before.

And it didn't take much to guess why he was in such high spirits. At his side walked the most beautiful girl I had ever seen.

As I watched her coming toward me I realized for the first time that tall could also be gorgeous. Even in her bare feet she was as tall as I was, but she moved with dazzling grace and self-assurance. I couldn't have pointed to her clothes, her makeup, her hair, and said exactly what it was that gave her that air of casual perfection, but whatever she did, she did it right.

"You just tell your mother to come by any time," Mr. Douglas was saying. "I've got a couple of picture frames she might like to have, too."

"Sure, I'll let her know," I said. But I was hardly listening. Roy had spotted me. He waved and hurried forward. I saw him touch the girl's arm, gently urging her to quicken her steps.

"Marcy, wait up," he called. "Hey, you weren't looking for me by any chance, were you?"

"No," I said, trying to keep my tone light.

"I was just out running a couple of errands."

"I want you to meet Kate," Roy said. "She just came up from New York for the weekend."

The girl smiled and held out her hand. Her nails were long and carefully tapered.

"From New York?" I repeated numbly. "You live there? Right in the city?"

"Well, Roy and I are really from the suburbs—Westchester County. But I've got a summer job in the city, with a magazine."

"I'm going to move along now." I'd almost forgotten about Mr. Douglas. "I won't bother you young folks. Enjoyed talking to you, Marcy."

"Me too," I said. I wished I could go on with him, could get him to distract me with old stories of Lake Marinac. But I couldn't tear myself away from Roy and Kate yet. I had to learn everything I could about her.

"What do you do—on the magazine, I mean?" I asked her.

Kate shrugged. "It's kind of boring, really. I'm learning to do layout."

I didn't know what layout was, but I certainly wasn't about to ask.

"I'm sharing an apartment with a friend of mine from college," she went on. "It's a sublet. That's the best thing about the summer, really being on my own."

I wasn't too sure what a sublet was, either, but I nodded and said it sounded great.

"I'm going to take Kate out in the boat," Roy said. "Poor kid, she's been cooped up in high-rises all summer. You want to come, Marcy?"

Are you out of your mind, I wanted to shout at him. Why would you want me tagging along when you've already got her? But I just shook my head, and said, "No, I've a lot of things to do."

"Oh, don't be so conscientious all the time," Roy said. "You're entitled to a little fun now and then."

"Not today," I said. It was back to the crossword puzzle for me today.

We were nearing the post office, and I decided that was as good a place as any for me to say good-bye. "See you guys later," I told them, turning in at the walk. "I've got to pick up the mail."

"Okay, if that's the way you want it," Roy said. "I'll be seeing you."

I crossed the wooden porch and entered the post office. The summer people always thought it was very picturesque, an old clapboard house that actually belonged to Mrs. Forbes, the postmistress. The front room served as the post office, and she and her elderly husband lived in back.

I nodded to Mrs. Forbes and hurried over to the mailboxes, knowing she'd try to detain me with all the latest Lake Marinac gossip.

There was something in our box, Box 90, but for a while I just stood looking through the little window, trying to put my thoughts in order. So Roy had a girlfriend from back home. And Kate wasn't just any girl. She was everything a boy could ever want—beautiful, intelligent, sophisticated. She was even a little older than he was, she had a certain worldly flair that would make her all the more exciting. So all of Roy's flirting with me and Eilene and however many other girls he'd met at Lake Marinac was only a game for him. The girl he really cared about was on a sublet, doing layout.

I'd never say so to Brian, but I'd have to admit to myself that he'd been right after all. Roy Lowell just wasn't ever going to pay much attention to me.

The screen door banged. I heard Mrs. Forbes' cheery "Good afternoon, what can I do for you?" and glanced around to see Mrs. Lowell approach the counter.

I twirled the combination, 1-4-3, and pulled open the door of our mailbox. There was a notice for a registered package. I would have to sign for it. It would be for Dad, I knew—he was always sending away for tools and things. I took the slip to the counter and waited behind Mrs. Lowell.

Mrs. Forbes was weighing a thick envelope. "That'll be fifty-two cents," she said. She studied the address. "To Santa Fe, New Mexico. That's really interesting. Ever been out there?"

It was amazing how much Mrs. Lowell and Kate looked alike. Kate was several inches taller, of course, but they had the same shining hair, the same flawless taste in clothes, the same poise—and the song "I want a girl just like the girl that married dear old dad" jangled through my head.

"We took the kids out there last summer," Mrs. Lowell said, counting out change.

"Oh, isn't that interesting," Mrs. Forbes exclaimed. "I got a brochure one time—from the travel people, you know—and there were such nice pictures of Indians and Mexican people and mountains."

"I have to go," said Mrs. Lowell, edging her way toward the door. "I've got a houseful this weekend."

"Oh, you've got company, have you? Who's visiting?"

Mrs. Lowell sighed with exasperation. "My husband and our daughter. They only get up here every few weekends."

"Oh, your husband and daughter." Mrs. Forbes' face brightened at this tidbit of information. I knew she'd be passing it along to everyone who came into the post office for the rest of the afternoon: the rest of the Lowell family's up now, haven't you met them yet? Yes, the husband and the daughter. . . .

"Now I know your son, that's Roy—such a nice, polite fellow, you must be so proud of him. And your daughter, what's her name?"

"Kate," Mrs. Lowell called over her shoulder as she made her escape. It was a good thing she didn't give a backward glance, because she would have seen me staring after her with my mouth hanging open.

"Now, Marcy, sorry I kept you waiting," Mrs. Forbes said. "Oh, yes, there's a package for your dad."

I signed the form and she handed me a flat heavy box from behind the counter. She tried to guess what might be inside. She asked me if Mom had gotten over her cold, and if Dad had put out the buoys so the sailboat races could begin Sunday morning. But at last I got away.

I could have been jubilant, but I wasn't. I could have skipped down the road and rushed out to the Lowells' dock and tried to catch Roy and Kate before they took off in the boat, but I didn't.

As I walked slowly back toward home what I felt mostly was ashamed of myself. I couldn't believe that I'd been silly enough to get all upset over the thought that Roy might have a girlfriend down in the city. And now that all my fears had come to nothing, I was left dazed and empty, wondering why it had all seemed so important to me in the first place.

Yes, Roy was special. He wasn't like the small-town boys I had met at Callonville Regional. He came from a different world, a world where people traveled and read and took all the finer things in life for granted. Sometimes, talking to Carmen Calderón or playing some piece by Bach or Rodrigo, I felt as though the world were so close I could almost brush it with my fingertips. But when I was with Roy and the others who came to Lake Marinac as a retreat from their busy exciting lives in the city, I could believe that the world I dreamed of was within my grasp.

And there was something else. Roy was fun to be with, he made me feel feminine and attractive in spite of my height. I couldn't forget how he'd come into the store just to help me pass the time, or the way he always called me "Marci-oh," or how our hands touched as we sat on the stern seat in the outboard. It had taken me all week to get up the nerve to accept his water-skiing invitation, but he'd been in my thoughts a lot these past few days, more than I liked to admit to myself.

Every time I set out from the house I hoped I might meet him on the street. Whenever I was alone, I had long conversations with him inside my head. Now I had to face the truth. It went beyond any of the reaons I could think of, but I was hooked on Roy Lowell.

It was one thing to admit that I had become interested in Roy. It was harder to admit to myself that I had become totally shameless where he was concerned.

But here I stood at the Lowells' screen door, holding the pair of sunglasses Mrs. Lowell had left behind her on the counter at the store this morning. We could have called her to let her know we had them, and she could have picked them up at her leisure. But, no—I had to jump at the chance to go over to the Lowells'. Already as I waited on the front steps I was imagining that Roy would open the door, would greet me with surprise and delight, would invite me in. . . .

I knocked again, my ears sharpened to catch every telltale sound from within the house. What if he just thanked me and took the glasses and shut the door again? That was what I deserved for all my scheming.

Water was running somewhere inside, and I decided they probably couldn't hear my knock. "Anybody home?" I called.

There was silence for a second or two, then footsteps hurried toward me and Mrs. Lowell appeared in the doorway to the screened-in porch. "Oh, Marcy," she said. "Hello, what can I do for you?"

She looked as though she were going to address a Woman's Club luncheon. Her pants suit was straight out of *Vogue*, her nails were manicured and every strand of hair was in place. I wondered if she ever went around in old work shirts and paint-spattered pants like normal people.

"You were looking for me or for Roy?" she asked, jolting me back to my mission.

"Oh, for you," I said too quickly. "You forgot these at the store, so I brought them over." I held out the glasses in their tooled-leather case.

"Oh, thank you." Her smile expanded and for the first time I felt that she had really seen me. "How sweet of you. I'd have been hunting all day."

I tried to peer in past her shoulder, but there was no sign of Roy. Most likely he was out on the lake somewhere. It was ridiculous for me to be thinking about him so much. "Oh, that's okay," I said. "I was coming past here anyway."

I turned to go, but Mrs. Lowell went on, "I don't know what's the matter with me lately, I'm getting so scatterbrained."

I must have stared at her in amazement. "You?" I exclaimed. "I'd never think of you as scatterbrained—you're always so composed."

"Well, thanks, Marcy," she said, and she almost laughed. "I'm glad somebody thinks I'm efficient. I think I've just got too many things on my mind at once lately, especially now that I'm on this committee to organize the *Scandals*."

"The *Marinac Scandals*?" I repeated. "You mean that show they put on every August?"

She nodded. "I thought I came up here to get away from it all, and here I am again. . . ." She paused, as though struck by a sudden thought. "Come in and sit down a minute, I'll tell you about it."

I couldn't imagine why she would want to discuss the *Scandals*, or anything else, with me. But obediently I stepped onto the porch and pulled the screen door shut behind me. I took one of the fan-backed wicker chairs and Mrs. Lowell sat down across from me. Between us stood a round glass-topped table with a vase of dried flowers.

"Yes, I volunteered to be on the committee," she resumed when we were settled. "In fact, it looks as though I'm the chairwoman. So I have to get the program together, have the publicity taken care of, get the tickets printed and sold, make sure the community house is set up. . . ."

She paused, and I felt I should be making some comment. "It sounds like a lot of work to me," I said.

"It won't be too bad if I delegate properly," she said, crossing one slender ankle over the other. "That's what makes a good chairperson, isn't it—the ability to delegate responsibility?"

"I guess so. I never really thought about it." A pair of water skis leaned in a far corner of the porch. So Roy wasn't out skiing then. He might be sitting on the dock, though, with Bob Hansen or Eilene. . . .

"The trouble is," Mrs. Lowell went on, "this is our first summer here, you know. I

still don't know very many people yet, so
it's hard for me to approach people and ask
them to help out. But it just occurred to
me—well, I know your father and mother
are very busy with the store and everything, but do you think they might find a
little extra time to pitch in?"

Suddenly I understood why she had decided to talk to me. I shook my head. "I
don't think so," I said. "They really are
awfully busy during the summer."

I could just hear Dad if he ever found out
she'd dared to make such a suggestion:
Isn't it enough that we have to unstop their
plumbing and mend their roofs and chase
away bats for them? Now they expect us to
entertain them, too?

Mrs. Lowell sighed. "That's what I was
afraid of. Mrs. Murphy's going to help out
with the program; she knows most of the
people who've been in it the past couple of
years. But there are still so many things to
do. What was the show like last year,
Marcy? What kinds of skits did they do?"

"I don't really know," I said. "I didn't go."

"You didn't?" Mrs. Lowell exclaimed.
"But I thought everybody went."

Not everybody, I wanted to tell her.
Maybe all the summer people went, but my
family didn't, and neither did the Townsends, nor Mr. Douglas, nor the Van Horns
from down at the North Shore—in fact,
none of the year-rounders would bother to
go except Mrs. Forbes from the post office,

who was afraid to miss anything, especially anything called *Scandals*.

But instead I said, "I heard they used a live goat in one of the skits. I don't know why, exactly, but it got loose and went running through the audience. . . ."

She laughed, but the laugh had a little shudder in it somewhere. "Well, we won't have any livestock this year," she said. "Not as long as I'm in charge."

There was another long pause. Those wicker chairs were pretty, but they certainly weren't comfortable.

"So your parents are out, then," Mrs. Lowell said. "All right, I won't even bother asking them about it. I've gotten Roy to promise he'll help out here and there of course, and he's supposed to get some of his friends involved. Maybe you could work with them, Marcy, selling tickets and things like that. It really wouldn't take much time."

But year-rounders didn't enter the sailboat races or weigh in the fish we caught for the annual fishing contest. We didn't join in their mock Olympic swimming races or attend their masquerade party. And we certainly had nothing to do with that silly collection of skits and song-and-dance routines which, for some unknown reason, they had always called the *Marinac Scandals*.

"Well," I said, "it does sound like fun. I

think I'd have time to help out a little, anyway."

Because where Roy Lowell was concerned I had become totally shameless.

"No, I'm not objecting," Dad said. "It's entirely up to you. It's just that you'll probably regret it once you get involved with those people, and then you won't be able to get out of it gracefully."

I put down the ear of corn I'd been gnawing on and gave him what I hoped was a withering look across the dinner table. "What's the difference between that and objecting?" I asked pointedly.

"Well, okay, you've got me there," he said, managing a laugh. "But you understand how things are around here, don't you? In the summer we're working people, and apart from our work we're supposed to keep kind of a low profile, you know what I mean?"

I knew what he meant, all right, but I didn't know of any law that said it had to be that way.

I turned to Mom, who had been sitting quietly concentrating on her plate. "I just thought it'd be fun to try it," I told her. "What have I got to lose?"

Mom sighed. "I'm not sure it's such a good idea," she said. "I don't want to discourage you, but—"

I should have known she'd side with Dad.

I banged down my fork in disgust. "How can you figure I'm going where I'm not wanted when Mrs. Lowell just about begged me to help out?" I exclaimed.

Mom's finger traced a rose on the flowered tablecloth. She never liked to speak ill of people, even of people she didn't like especially. So I knew she couldn't quite bring herself to say what was on her mind— that even though Mrs. Lowell wanted my help, somehow that wasn't quite the same thing as wanting me. Somehow, Mom was thinking, Mrs. Lowell and the rest of the summer people would let me know that I wasn't quite in their league.

But Mom just pushed back her chair and went out to the kitchen for the dessert. And that might have been the end of it if Brian, after staying away nearly two weeks, hadn't had to choose that very moment to arrive at the back door.

"Come on in, stranger," Mom called, and Brian clattered into the kitchen. "You're just in time for blueberry pie."

"Trust me to show up for that," Brian said, grinning his old grin.

It was good to see him again. I felt almost shy as we said hello to each other in the kitchen. I didn't quite know what to say to him as we carried out the dessert dishes and the coffee together. I didn't want to talk about his long absence, but it wasn't something I could pretend away, either.

"Well, how's life under the Golden Arches?" I asked as he pulled up a chair to join us at the table.

"Oh, they finally broke up," Brian said cheerfully.

"Who?" I demanded, bewildered.

"Louise, my boss. She got the crucial phone call from her boyfriend this morning. And today was supposed to be good for Virgo, too. Julie went around singing, 'O willow, titwillow, titwillow,' all day."

We both laughed and I began to relax. Maybe, after all, nothing had changed.

"I just thought I ought to drop by and tell you Tom killed another copperhead this morning," Brian said, turning to Dad. "Right on the path about halfway to the cove."

"Let's hope it's *the* other one," Dad said. "They haven't been too bad this year, really."

So that was why Brian had come, I thought with a twinge of disappointment. He'd just dropped by on business, not because he wanted to see me. I wished he would flash me a smile to let me know we were still friends, but he dug into his wedge of pie as if he hadn't eaten all day.

On any other evening we could have lapsed into a long talk about Mr. Townsend's new novel or the quality of the fishing this year. But the *Marinac Scandals* hadn't been laid to rest. "Ask Brian," Dad said suddenly. "Find out what he thinks about all this."

I didn't have to find out, but naturally Brian threw me a questioning glance that couldn't be ignored, and I had to explain everything.

"Well, we're right where we left off," he said when I finished, and I knew what he meant. "Sure, I don't see why you shouldn't mess around at the *Scandals*. It's your decision."

We went on talking about other things after that, but I felt uneasy, as if I'd done something wrong and pretty soon I'd have to pay the price. Finally Dad offered to help Mom with the dishes and Brian and I wandered out onto the front porch. We had one of those old-fashioned porch swings that are supposed to be so romantic, but now, as Brian and I sat down on it, we pressed into opposite corners with a couple of pillows and old magazines between us as a buffer.

"Okay," I said. "I can't stand it. Will you tell me what's bugging you?"

"You know what it is," Brian said. "Why do I have to explain anything?"

"You have to explain," I said carefully, "why I haven't got the freedom to do what I want and be with whomever I want to be with."

Brian gave a shove with his foot that got the swing going crooked. It bumped against the support pole every time it swung back.

"Go where you want, do what you want," he grumbled. "Just don't require me to like it, that's all."

I picked up one of the pillows and turned it between my hands. Grandma Galaway had made it and there was a big G embroidered in one corner.

"You know, I just realized something," I said after a while. "You and Mom and Dad—just about all the year-rounders, I guess—are always accusing the summer people of being snobbish. So you look down on them, you don't associate with them, you make fun of them behind their backs. So really you're just as snobbish as you say they are. Probably even worse."

It was a real revelation, and for just an instant even Brian was shocked. But, of course, he made an immediate recovery. "If we are, it's in self-defense," he said, "because you know who started it. By the way, Roy isn't working on the *Scandals* by any chance, is he?"

"He's helping out a little. So what?"

Brian shrugged. "It just figures, that's all."

"You just wait," I exclaimed. "I'm going to have a really good time, and then you'll see I was right."

But Brian always had to have the last word. "If the summer people were some kind of food," he said, "you know what it'd be? One of those soufflés that comes out of the oven all puffed up and beautiful, till you stick a fork in it and the whole thing collapses. There's nothing in it, just a lot of steam comes out."

"Oh, Brian, stop it," I said. But the trouble was I couldn't help laughing.

6

"Three-forty-six," I told Mr. Douglas. I slipped his coffee, sugar and Scotch tape into a bag, counted out his change and glanced up to see who was next in line.

I looked straight up into the grinning face of Roy Lowell.

I struggled to sound very ordinary and businesslike as I asked, "Can I help you with anything?" But my heart was doing very peculiar things.

"Yeah," Roy said. "I need a couple paintbrushes, some cans of paint, some turpentine and—oh, yeah—two extra hands."

For half a second I just looked at him, bewildered, before I caught the joke. "Oh, yeah? Whose did you have in mind?"

"Yours. My mother says you offered to help with the *Scandals*. I'm supposed to be getting some of the kids together for a committee, so you're my first member."

"What do we have to paint?" I asked. I tried to sound nonchalant, as if I would consider putting in the time only if it were for a really worthwhile cause.

Roy shrugged. "They're lining up a couple of skits and they have to have a table and some chairs, and I guess there's a bookcase or something."

"When?" I asked. "When were you planning to do it?" After all, I wanted to imply, I had a very busy schedule, and I'd love to, but . . .

"Right now. Are you free?"

"Dad, can you come up front?" I shouted. "I'm going out for a while."

It wasn't until we had banged out the screen door that I remembered I was supposed to be playing it cool. I guess when Roy said "Right now" it just drove every other thought out of my head.

Like most of the houses at Lake Marinac, the Lowells' cottage didn't have much of a backyard. A white picket fence hemmed in a strip of grass and help back the tangle of bushes and underbrush that was the edge of the woods.

The furniture stood in a forlorn little cluster under a tree by the fence. Roy tossed me a frayed old shirt to wear as a smock and I dragged over a wooden crate to sit on.

"You may as well start with that table,"
Roy said. "What color do you want?"

I selected the can of red paint and soon
we were both at work. It was funny how I
forgot to worry about what to say when my
hands were busy. I swished a broad red
stripe along the far edge of the table, dipped
my brush again and watched the stripe
grow even wider. And suddenly, before I
knew the question was about to pop out, I
heard myself asking, "Are you going to be a
senior this year?"

"Yeah," Roy said. "What about you?"

"I'll just be a junior," I said. "Two more
years to go. It feels like forever."

"Can't wait to get it over with, huh?"

I slapped a vehement red swath across
the tabletop. "I sure can't," I said. "I don't
know where I'll go once I graduate, but I'm
not going to hang around here the rest of my
life."

"Why not?" Roy asked in surprise. "Lots
of people I know back home are dying to get
out to places like this. It seems to me you've
got it made."

"You've got to be kidding," I exclaimed.
"Stuck away up here where nothing ever
happens and you see the same old people
day after day?"

Roy half-turned away from me to reach
the back of the chair he was painting. "I
guess the thing is," he said after a while,
"wherever you're from, you always want to
get away and try something different."

"Well, what about you?" I demanded. "Talk about having it made—you live right there so close to New York you can just go into the city anytime you want. You wouldn't want to change that, would you?"

"Maybe not permanently," he admitted. "But I'm sure looking forward to getting away to college. It's like the first step toward really being on my own, you know?"

I nodded. I knew, all right. "Where are you going to go? Have you figured that out yet?"

"I'd like to go to Yale," Roy said dreamily. "But I doubt if I'll get in there. Dad went to Northwestern and I've got a feeling that's where I'll end up. And it doesn't really matter that much where I go, I just have to go somewhere, away from home."

I dipped my brush again and scraped off the excess paint. How could he talk so casually about going to schools like Yale and Northwestern? I'd be lucky if I could just go away to State. Roy really did come from another world—and yet here I sat talking to him in the backyard just as easily as I might talk to Brian or Kathy.

I wanted to hear everything about his home, his plans, the places he'd been and the people he'd known. I wished there were a hundred more tables for us to paint so the afternoon could stretch on forever.

"I bet you're the kind of person that knows exactly what you want to do with your life," I said. "Not like me."

"I don't know what ever gave you that idea," Roy said with a short laugh. "The only thing I'm sure of is what I don't want to be. I don't want to be a stockbroker like my father—it's just too cutthroat, I couldn't stand it. Apart from that, I guess I'm open to suggestions."

Could this be the same carefree teasing Roy Lowell who pretended he was going to ram our canoe? He was letting me see a different side of himself this afternoon.

"You could be a doctor," I said. "Or a laywer. Or an Indian chief."

We both giggled. "Hey, that'd be great," Roy said. "Can't you just see me going home for the weekend in beaded moccasins and a feathered war bonnet, with a string of scalps on my belt?"

I liked laughing with him, too. But when the picture faded, I asked, "Seriously, though, what do you think you'd like?"

"You mean really?" Roy paused, as though he were debating whether to share his thoughts with me. "You know what I'd really like to do? I'd like to learn how to design buildings—you know, study architecture. But it's a long course—it takes almost as long as it does to become a doctor."

"I never knew anybody who was an architect," I said. I couldn't conceal the trace of awe that crept into my voice, that living proof that I was just a hick from out in the sticks.

But Roy didn't seem to notice. "They've

got the technology to build almost anything these days," he said. "But most of the time it seems like they don't have any imagination, or else they just don't care. You look at the buildings going up in New York, unbelievably ugly, some of them. They spend millions of dollars on something that—"

"Hey! Hey, Roy!"

I froze, my paintbrush in midair. A little blob of paint slid off the tip onto the grass like a big red tear.

"Eilene!" Roy dropped his brush and sprang to his feet. "Come on, we're back here."

Eilene rounded the corner of the house, her sandals slapping along the flagstone walk. "Man, I looked all *over* for you!" she told Roy. "I went down to your dock, and over to Bob's house, and nobody even knew where you were."

"That's what they always say," Roy said. "A good man is hard to find."

"Hi, Marcy." Eilene turned to me almost as an afterthought. "Hey, what are you guys doing anyhow? Painting?"

I felt like saying, No, we're drilling a hole to China. But I just nodded and said, "Yeah, for the *Scandals*."

"I forgot to tell you," Roy said, "you're on the *Scandals* committee, Eilene. Grab a brush."

"Who says?" Eilene backed away, hiding her hands behind her. "I didn't come over here to work."

"Oh, yeah? That's what you think!" Roy lunged for her and grabbed her by the shoulder. Eilene gave a little scream that turned into a giggle. She didn't try very hard at all to get away. "Nobody gets out of here without contributing." Roy laughed. "Right, Marcy?"

"Right," I said. I felt big and awkward and dull. Everything had changed so fast. A minute ago Roy had been confiding in me as if I were someone special, a soulmate. But now that Eilene had appeared, I had somehow faded into the background.

What did Eilene have that I was lacking? Did Roy like her because she was prettier and funnier than I was? Or was it that she was more like him, one of the summer people, part of that world I had never entered?

Protesting all the while, Eilene finally accepted a paintbrush and set to work on the little bookcase. She couldn't even decide what color to use without Roy's help. From the way she acted, you'd think she had never painted before in her life.

I touched up the last spots on the table and stepped back to survey the finished product.

"That looks pretty good," Roy said. "You're just getting into gear. You start out with one little table and pretty soon you'll be painting the town red."

I didn't think it was very funny. I barely managed a polite laugh, but Eilene burst into a fountain of giggles. "Oh, Roy!" she exclaimed. "I can't get into all these little corners with this big brush. Come here, look."

Roy hovered over her, helping her, joking with her. It was hard to believe he was the same person who had just told me his dream of studying architecture. I felt as though Eilene had come and stolen the wonderful moments Roy and I had shared.

But Roy didn't resent Eilene's interruption. If anything, he seemed to welcome it. He had stepped right back into his old character. Eilene had launched into some story about an air mattress with a leak in it, and Roy rocked back on his heels and laughed. Nothing I said ever made him laugh like that.

Noisy and meaningless, their words rattled against my ears. I couldn't understand what they were talking about. I wondered if I even spoke their language.

"Oh, Marcy, you're not going already?" Roy asked as I went to the outdoor tap and rinsed my paintbrush.

"I better get back to the store," I said. "My father didn't expect me to be gone very long."

"But you're going to help sell tickets, aren't you?" Roy wanted to know. "My mother said you would."

I thought of what Mom and Dad had said. I remembered Brian's warnings. And here it was, just like they'd told me. I could help out, but I wasn't quite acceptable as one of them, as a friend. If Roy had his choice between me and Eilene, it was clear where I stood.

Maybe I was reacting too much. After all, no one had purposely done anything to try to hurt my feelings. But listening to Roy and Eilene chatter away so happily, I couldn't help the way I felt.

"I'll have to see if I've got time," I said, and I walked out to the road without a backward glance.

"I've decided that knowing Roy is nothing but a source of frustration and disappointment," I concluded my long outpouring letter to Kathy in Maine. "I just can't stand having him be nice one minute—acting like he really likes me and I'm special to him or something—and then dropping me the next. I don't know if he's really interested in Eilene or what, but anyway I guess I don't really have a chance with him. Now I've just got to convince myself it's good riddance to bad rubbish."

There was nobody else I could tell but Kathy, and she was so far away it didn't seem to help much. The only thing that would really make me feel any better would be to push Roy out of my thoughts. And the best way to do that would be to lose myself in playing the guitar.

By now it was hard to remember why I'd once worried so much about that waltz by

Fernando Sor. Today my fingers sprinted up and down through all the intricate turns of the melody. The piece would really be mine soon. It would become part of me like the Bach preludes I had learned by heart.

I finished with a flourish and clapped for myself, beaming at myself in the mirror above the bureau. I couldn't wait for my lesson Thursday afternoon. Even Carmen Calderón would have to admit I was improving.

I slid my left hand up and down the fret board in a series of diminished chords. I floated through three- or four-finger exercises, and then, sitting tall and resolute, the music on the stand before me, I dived into the waltz again.

Usually Mom was careful not to interrupt when I was practicing. Now the knock on my door snapped my concentration. I lost my place in the music and broke off in the middle of the second variation. "What?" I called, none too graciously.

Mom opened the door a couple of inches and peered in at me. "I'm sorry," she said. "I hate to interrupt you, but Mrs. Lowell's here and she insisted she had to talk to you."

"What's Mrs. Lowell doing here?" I asked in surprise.

"Oh, she got a letter of ours in her mail by mistake, so she brought it over." Mom lowered her voice. "I tried to tell her you were practicing, but you know how she won't take no for an answer."

I knew all right. I put my guitar down on the bed and stood up. "Okay," I said. "I guess I better see what she wants. She's probably going to ask me to make posters or something."

Mrs. Lowell looked a little bit out of place on our front porch with Dad's fishing poles and tackle box, the potted herbs Mom kept meaning to replant in the garden, and the usual scattering of old newspapers and magazines. But she came forward smiling when she saw me. "Marcy," she exclaimed. "Here I've been hunting all over for people with talent, and you were right here all along."

So it wasn't about posters, then. Still I pretended I didn't know what was coming, stalling for time. "Me?" I asked blankly. "What do you mean?"

"I thought it was a record," she said. "But then your mother said no, that you'd been studying for years."

I turned to glare at Mom over my shoulder, and she looked away with a guilty half-smile.

"I'm not very good yet," I said. "There are still chords I can hardly even reach."

"Don't be modest," Mrs. Lowell said. "I heard you from out here. You can't deny the evidence of my own ears."

I didn't know what to say. I stood with my

hands knotted at my sides, shifting from one bare foot to the other.

"So as soon as I heard you, I got the idea," she went on. "You could play a piece or two in the *Scandals*. You could—"

"Oh, no, please," I burst out. "I really couldn't—I never played in front of an audience, not ever."

Mrs. Lowell put on her brightest, most charming smile. "There's got to be a first time," she said.

"Anyway," I went on, groping frantically for a better argument, "the *Scandals* is always light. People want funny skits, little humorous songs and dances, things like that. I'd be completely out of place."

"I don't agree with you at all," Mrs. Lowell said. "In a show there should be changes of mood; it's the best way to keep the audience interested."

She was like a sewing machine, I thought: every time I found a hole through which I could escape, she stitched it up. I looked back at Mom, who stood in the doorway trying to keep out of things. I wished she would step in with some excuse that couldn't be questioned. If only she'd say that performing was against my religion or something. But Mom must have decided this was my own decision. If I was so fond of the summer people, she was probably thinking, maybe I'd actually like to play in the *Scandals*.

"I just can't, that's all," I said. "I'm just not ready, I'm sorry."

"I am, too," Mrs. Lowell said, turning to go. "You really could add something special."

"Thank you for bringing that letter," Mom said.

"Oh, that's all right," said Mrs. Lowell. "You think about it, though, Marcy. If you change your mind, let me know."

"Okay," I said, and watched her down the front steps and out to the road.

Mom dropped onto the swing. "Well, I'm surprised you didn't want to be in the show, Marcy. The way you've been getting so involved in things lately."

I didn't want to tell her I couldn't bear being in the *Scandals* knowing I'd have to watch Roy and Eilene flirting backstage through all the rehearsals. It was tough enough admitting to myself that I'd made a mistake about Roy, maybe about summer people in general. I couldn't stand to listen to "I told you so" too.

"I'm not good enough to perform yet," I said. "Miss Calderón would have a fit if I did a thing like that. I'd be getting too big for my britches."

Mom gave the swing a little push. "You know, I've got a feeling about that Mrs. Lowell. Somehow I think she gets people to do what she wants in the end."

"Well, she's not getting me to do any-

thing," I declared. "Right now I've got a
date with Fernando Sor."

It was late afternoon when I finally got
out to our dock. There was still plenty of
sun, and the light breeze teased the water
into ripples. I had brought a book—I was in
the middle of a good Agatha Christie—but I
didn't open it. I stretched out in a canvas
beach chair and closed my eyes. I liked the
sound of the water lapping against the poles
that supported the dock. When I was little, I
used to lie with my ear against the planks
and drop pebbles into the lake to hear the
strange hollow music they made, each
stone sounding a different note.

I was lucky to live at Lake Marinac, I
thought. I had the lake, the hills and the
clear air. Sometimes there was the dazzling
blue sky, and sometimes there was the
thrill of watching a squall sweep down the
lake. I had friends—Brian, of course, and
Kathy, and kids I knew from school. So why
should I have begun to feel so restless? Why
did I keep longing for something more?

Growing pains, Mom would call it. I'd get
over it. I'd learn to be satisfied with everything I had, instead of craving things I
didn't know anything about.

But suppose I was really meant for a
different kind of life—for the concert stage,
maybe . . . for champagne and speeding
taxis and the lilt of exotic languages . . . for
adventure? How would I ever find my way

from Lake Marinac to the place where I truly belonged? I had hoped that Roy Lowell might hold the key I needed, but now I would have to start looking all over again.

I must have felt the deep throbbing of the planks beneath me before my mind finally registered that someone was coming. When I looked up at last, I sat bolt upright, so startled no words would come to my rescue. Striding toward me down the dock was Roy Lowell.

"Don't get up, Sleeping Beauty," he said, dropping down beside my chair. "You look fine where you are."

"Roy!" I exclaimed. "You startled me. I mean, I didn't know it was you."

"You're never safe," he said. "I turn up when you least expect it."

He stretched out on his stomach, leaning on his elbows to watch me. I noticed that he had lost his city pallor during the last weeks, and he glowed with a healthy golden tan.

"Well, what brings you out here?" I asked. Maybe I sounded a little cool, but I couldn't look at him without remembering him and Eilene. From now on I'd be on my guard.

"What makes you think I've got a specific errand?" Roy asked. "Maybe I just came by to see you. I haven't seen you around for a couple of days, you know."

"I've been kind of busy," I said. But I could feel myself weakening already.

"You shouldn't work so hard," Roy said. "Take some lessons from me. I just laze around and enjoy life."

He lay on the sun-warmed dock like a big contented cat, I thought. And just like a cat he made me feel honored that he had chosen to be with me. Maybe he only giggled and flirted with Eilene, while with me he revealed his deeper feelings. . . .

"How come you never told me you play classical guitar?" he asked suddenly. "My mother just told me she heard you this afternoon."

I could feel my cheeks flush hot. "I was right," I said. "You did have a reason to come out here. But I already explained to her."

Roy sat up and gave me his most open, direct smile. "Well, maybe I did," he said. "That's okay, isn't it?"

And all I could answer was, "Sure, it's okay."

"I took trumpet for a year," he went on, "but I didn't have much of an ear for it. My mother says you sounded really good. Professional."

I was blushing more than ever. "I guess she couldn't hear me too well from out on the porch," I said.

"I'd like to hear you play sometime," Roy said. Now his voice was almost shy. "Maybe sometime I could come by and listen to whatever you're working on."

We could sit on the porch swing and I

would play him the waltz and the preludes, and the swing would rock gently back and forth, and Roy would tell me about his friends and the places he's been and the things he wants to do someday. I would play very softly as he talked, and he would turn to gaze into my face. . . .

"Sure," I said, before my fantasy could get totally out of hand. "You could come by some evening."

"I'll do that." He smiled. "But, about the *Scandals* . . ."

Why did he have to bring up the *Scandals* again? But now I didn't protest. I listened almost eagerly to everything he had to say.

"I can see why you said no," Roy said. "You might feel out of place if the show was like it has been in the past. But this year it's going to be a little different."

"Different? How?"

"With my mother in charge it'll be different." Roy laughed. "For one thing, she wants more variety. Like, for instance, she's getting the Spaldings—you know, the husband and wife that have been on Broadway—to do a reading, some scene from *Hedda Gabler*, I think. That'll be somewhere in the second half. And right before the intermission she wants a musical interlude. You know Liz, don't you? Liz Schneider. She plays the flute, and I got thinking maybe the two of you could work out a duet."

"You mean I wouldn't have to play alone up there?"

"No, you'll have company. And I'll be backstage to hold your hand before you go on. Is that a deal?"

I had to turn away so he wouldn't see my face. I didn't want him to guess how much power he had over me. But in that moment I knew that if Roy wanted me to perform a series of backward somersaults across the stage, I'd go home and start practicing on the carpet.

"It'd have to be something pretty simple," I said. "We've only got what—about three and a half weeks?"

"Till August eighteenth," he said. "You can do it, though. You'll work out something."

I tried to picture Liz—silky honey-brown hair and a friendly smile. Hadn't she said something about how nice it must be up here in the winter? And if she cared about music, maybe we could find something in common. "Have you talked to Liz about all this?" I asked.

"She'll do it," Roy assured me. "If I ask her, she'll do it."

A fresh breeze kicked up the surface of the lake and little waves lapped against the dock. "Okay, I'll be in the *Scandals*," I promised. "We'll figure out something. It sounds like fun."

7

"What was all that she said about the rehearsal starting promptly at seven-thirty?" Liz muttered. "Let's get the show on the road."

Judging from the bedlam backstage in the community house, I suspected that the first rehearsal for the *Marinac Scandals* wasn't going to get under way for hours. Mr. Murphy, the saxophonist with the jazz combo, had just run home for a new package of reeds. Mrs. Murphy had insisted that the twins be given parts as Indians in the opening skit, "Washington Crossing Lake Marinac." They darted out of corners and wriggled under furniture with earsplitting war whoops, brandishing their rubber tomahawks. Mr. Abano, who was to be George Washington, sat on a wooden stool with a pipestem between his teeth, blowing smoke rings as though he didn't care if the roof collapsed around him. The famous Broadway Spaldings, Ed and Margot, were supposed to do a scene from *Hedda Gabler*. But they must have had a fight before they came to rehearsal, because now they sulked in opposite corners, glaring and refusing to speak to each other. Roy, the stage manager, still hadn't shown up to raise the curtain and work the lights.

But at last Mrs. Lowell called back to us from the stage. "All right, everybody. I don't know where my son is—I'll hang him by his thumbs when he gets here—and Art Flannery's our master of ceremonies and he couldn't get here till eight. But we're getting started anyway. So there'll be a little introduction, just a few words about the show, and then we'll begin at the beginning with George Washington. George, you're on."

"Who, me?" Mr. Abano came to life. He jumped up and overturned a music stand with a tremendous crash. "I thought—I didn't realize . . ."

"How did I do it?" Liz groaned. "How did I get myself into this?"

"*They* got us into it," I reminded her. "Roy and his mother. I feel I had nothing to do with it."

"Well, thank goodness we don't have to come to every rehearsal," said Liz. "Mrs. Lowell told me she won't really have to have us here till the last week."

"The main thing is we better practice together in between," I said. We had found a transcription for flute and guitar of Bach's "Jesu Joy of Man's Desiring." We had played it through yesterday afternoon over at Liz's place, and I knew instantly that she was really good. I only hoped I could measure up to her.

There was a burst of giggles and the backstage door flew open. In came Eilene, her hands full of parcels. Right at her heels, carrying two six-packs of Coke, sauntered Roy. "They started?" he exclaimed in amazement. "I thought it wasn't till eight."

Some excuse, I thought grimly. All the rest of us got here on time. Mrs. Lowell's own son would have to know that the rehearsal started at seven-thirty. But probably Roy and Eilene had been off having so much fun somewhere they forgot all about the time.

I reached behind me and touched the little table with its shiny coat of fresh red paint. Could I pretend that the afternoon behind the Lowells' cottage had never happened?

From beyond the flimsy partition that separated us from the stage Mr. Abano exclaimed, "The troops will need provisions, Martha! Where did you pack the hamburger rolls?" It was the kind of line that would probably bring down the house.

Roy stepped around a pile of boxes to

hand Liz and me each a Coke. "I'm gonna catch it, aren't I?" he whispered.

I nodded. "Your mother said something about some sort of cruel and unusual punishment," I warned him.

Roy shrugged. "I guess with everything else she's got on her mind she'll forget all about it."

"Martha!" shouted George Washington. "What's that noise? I'm scared. It might be Indians."

The Murphy twins heard their cue and dashed for the door stage left. One of them tripped over a trailing shoelace and made his entrance sprawling across the stage. There was a howl and a flurry of anxious questions, and "Washington Crossing Lake Marinac" crashed to a halt.

Roy took advantage of the chaos to make his own discreet entrance. I heard his mother demand, "And where on earth have *you* . . ." before Martha Washington, played by Mrs. Hansen, interrupted her with a question about one of her lines.

"Pretzels, potato chips," Eilene chanted, wandering among the disgruntled cast members backstage. "Potato chips—bet you can't eat just one."

She was supposed to be helping make posters, which seemed pretty unlikely to me, considering how she'd acted when we were painting furniture. Probably she just used that as an excuse to hang around here with Roy.

The Spaldings sat in their corners and glared.

"They're doing Ibsen?" Liz said in wonder. "They ought to be doing *Who's Afraid of Virginia Woolf?*"

I'd never seen that play, so I didn't know how to answer her. Suddenly the noise in that airless little room backstage was too much for me. I couldn't bear the sight of Eilene's bobbing red curls, and her voice as she hawked her pretzels cut right through me. "I'm going to sit outside," I told Liz. "We won't go on for forty-five minutes at this rate."

"Wait, I'll come with you." Liz grabbed her flute in its case and got to her feet. "Maybe we can even practice a little."

I was beginning to like Liz Schneider, I decided, as we maneuvered our Cokes and our instruments out the stage door. Outside, it was deliciously quiet. The air hummed with crickets. Gravel crunched under our feet as we made our way to the wooden picnic tables that stood behind the community house.

We settled down, and Liz got out her flute and fitted the sections together. "If they could see me now back at Interlocken," she said with a droll expression, rolling astonished eyes toward the heavens.

"Where's Interlocken?" I ventured.

"Michigan," she said. "It's a school with a summer music camp. I was going to go again this year, but I figured if I came up here with my folks instead, I could at least get to see Jack, my boyfriend down home, a couple of weekends. Still I kind of miss it. All the top high-school musicians are there from all over the country. You ought to go sometime."

"Me?" I exclaimed. Of course I'd never be good enough, and even if I were, it was bound to cost more than I could afford. But that Liz had even suggested such a thing filled me with a warm glow.

I tuned up the D string on my guitar, and very softly, so no one could hear us from inside the community house, we began the prelude. Liz's flute trilled and soared, and I feared that, beside her, my own playing limped and stumbled. I had never shared music this way with anyone before. The guitar would create a trellis to support the vine of the flute's notes, I thought, and I strove to play my very best.

"Hey, that wasn't bad," Liz said when we came to the end. "Let's try again, and see if we can pick up that opening a little. I was lagging, and it slowed us both down."

It was all worth it for this. For this opportunity to accompany Liz, to perfect our performance with painstaking care, I could withstand the opposition of my parents, I could suffer through Brian's disapproval, I could even endure the flirtations of Roy and Eilene.

"I'm probably the one who was lagging,"

I told Liz. "Okay, let's do it again, and this time—"

I broke off. Steps crunched on gravel, and a familiar voice floated to me. I caught a fragment of a sentence about "starting off on the wrong foot." What I saw through the twilight didn't make any sense—two forms approaching the stage door of the community house, two people who could only be Brian Townsend and his father.

"And what?" asked Liz. "What's the matter?"

"Nothing. I thought I saw somebody, that's all." Somehow I wrenched my mind back to the Bach prelude. "Yes, let's go through it once more."

For a moment they hesitated at the door. Then, as I plucked the opening chord, they disappeared inside. What could they possibly be doing at a *Scandals* rehearsal with all those summer people? But somehow I forced myself through the piece again. We took the opening more quickly, and I felt a little shiver of excitement as I listened to the intricate harmony we wove together.

By the time we got back inside, Ed and Margot Spalding had made up. Now they shared one corner, their hands interlaced, their voices a low murmur as they gazed into each other's eyes. Eilene and Roy feasted on potato chips and whispered behind their hands. Brian and his father were nowhere to be seen, and I wondered if my imagination had deceived me.

"I'm not sure when we go on, are you?" Liz asked me in a low voice.

"I guess they'll announce when it's our turn," I said.

Mr. Flannery, Eilene's father, must have arrived, for from the stage a man's voice introduced the next skit, explaining something about the time-honored tradition of hunting and fishing at Lake Marinac. "But there's also something called government regulation," he went on. "Let's go to a remote cove on the East Shore, and you'll see what I'm talking about."

They must have been standing around a corner of the partition ready to step onto the stage, for suddenly, sounding strangely hollow and loud, came Mr. Townsend's voice.

"You got a license to fish here, mister?"

And Brian's voice, full of indignation, replied, "A license! You mean to tell me I need a license just to catch fish?"

I stared around me, half-expecting everyone to be listening openmouthed. But nobody else seemed impressed or even very interested. Margot Spalding cooed, and one of the Murphy twins (Paul?) dropped a handful of marbles and dived after them across the floor.

But very slowly it became real to me. Brian and his father were acting in a skit. Whoever had written it had certainly had the Townsends in mind. Brian, the poacher, launched into his arguments with lines like "Is it true or is it not true . . ." And

anyone who knew Mr. Townsend at all
would appreciate the irony of casting him
as the game warden. In real life the game
warden was always dropping by to check up
on Mr. Townsend.

At last the poacher talked his way out of
his difficulties by inviting the warden home
for a dinner of fresh largemouth bass. Then
Mr. Flannery was saying, "And now, ladies
and gentlemen, a little change of pace. I
want to introduce two lovely young ladies
who will give us a very special treat
tonight . . ." and we were on.

We entered stage left just as Brian and
his father exited stage right. And I don't
know how I managed to find my way
through the prelude.

Mr. Townsend was gone when Liz and I
got offstage, but Brian waited for me by the
door. "Okay," I said, "what's going on?"

"What do you mean?" he asked with his
most infectious grin. He waved me outside
into the night.

"Come off it, Brian," I said. "I heard you
up there, violating all your principles—"

"Well, I'm entitled to a little inconsistency once in a while," Brian said. "Just because I've got principles, that doesn't mean
I have to be a slave to them."

We stood under the big oak tree beside the
community house. I gazed at Brian in the
half-light, utterly baffled. "All right, let me
backtrack a little," I said finally. "When I
went water-skiing with Roy and some of the

other summer kids, you were kind of disgusted, right?"

Brian nodded.

"And then, when you heard I was going to help out backstage, you didn't exactly approve of that either."

Again that solemn nod of the head.

"And I haven't even seen you since I decided to play the guitar in the show. But I was pretty well convinced you'd think that was the last straw."

"I did. It led me to take drastic measures."

"This is drastic, all right," I said. "I just don't get it. What on earth made you decide to do a skit in the *Scandals?*"

"If you can play Bach, why can't I do a skit?" he said lightly. "Maybe I got sick of holing up over at the house, decided to go out and tackle the great unknown—"

"I just can't believe it," I said, shaking my head. "I heard you and your dad out there and I still can't believe it."

"When I make a move, I make a bold move," Brian said. "How do you like my new image?"

"You make a great poacher," I said. "Who wrote the skit, anyway?"

"Me and Dad. We sat up till after midnight last night. You know, it wasn't even hard to talk him into it. I think he really enjoyed writing for just regular people for a change instead of for learned professors."

The door opened, and Eilene and Roy

came out. Eilene switched on a transistor radio, and the chirping of the crickets was buried by a jangling ad for acne cream.

I hoped Brian didn't notice that I winced in the darkness. I was glad when he suggested, "We don't have to hang around for the second half. I'll walk you home, okay?"

"Okay," I said, and he even insisted on carrying my guitar.

I thought I knew Brian so well, but maybe I'd really never understand him, I reflected as we walked along Lakefront Road, listening to our footsteps in the quiet of the evening. But at least he wasn't angry at me anymore for being in the *Scandals*, and for some reason that made me feel light and happy.

8

Brian and his father performed their skit, which Mrs. Lowell had entitled "A Fine Kettle of Fish," and the audience loved it. The community house rocked with laughter. Backstage, nursing my anxiety about going on next, I could barely hear the lines I knew so well by now.

Naturally Liz wasn't the least bit nervous. She'd given her first recital when she was nine, and I could tell she didn't really take the *Marinac Scandals* too seriously. Now she and Eilene watched Mrs. Lowell as she made up Ed and Margot Spalding for their grand appearance in the second half of the show. I had to admit that Eilene had made some very attractive posters—it seemed that she wasn't so helpless after all once she made up her mind to do something.

I tuned and retuned my guitar and hoped my fingers wouldn't turn to dough when I got out onstage.

Suddenly I sensed that someone stood behind me, and glanced around. Roy grinned and folded himself into a chair on my right.

"Remember what I promised you?" he asked.

I shook my head. Just then all I wanted to remember was "Jesu Joy of Man's Desiring."

"You don't?" Roy asked. "My feelings are hurt. I promised I'd hold your hand before you went on, to bolster your courage."

My hands fell away from the strings. "Yes," I said slowly. "It's coming back to me now."

"Well, all right, then." Roy reached over and his cool firm hand swallowed mine. In the first moment I think I just stared at him, disbelieving. My cheeks flushed and I felt the sudden bumping of my heart.

"So how do you feel?" Roy wanted to know. "You nervous?"

"Yes," I said. But I'd forgotten all about my performance. I was nervous about sitting there with Roy, about Roy holding my hand.

"Just play the way you always do," Roy said. "You'll be beautiful."

I noticed that Eilene had stepped away from the Spaldings. She watched us closely, and there was no hint of her usual buoyant smile. I stiffened under her sharp, discerning gaze and tried to pull my hand away from Roy.

But he held it tightly, and his fingers traced over my knuckles. "They'll love you," he went on. "You know, you and Liz look great up there. They'll know you're pros, both of you."

"She's a pro," I corrected him. "When they hear me, they'll think it's amateur night."

"Hey, Roy," Eilene broke in. "You gotta do the lights in a minute, don't forget."

Through the rolling laughter of the audience I sifted Brian's voice: "Oh, don't worry about those. Maybe you'd like to drop by for a little country cooking." The skit was almost over.

Roy gave my hand a parting squeeze. "Good luck," he whispered as he got to his feet.

The community house shook with applause. How could Liz and I follow an act like that, I wondered. People wanted to slap their knees and laugh till tears ran down their cheeks. They didn't come to the *Scandals* to listen to Bach.

But maybe Roy had given me courage, just as he promised. I felt strangely calm as Liz and I waited at the door stage left. Mr. Flannery, the master of ceremonies, recited the lines we'd heard every night that week: "I want to introduce two lovely young ladies who will give us a very special treat tonight—Liz Schneider and Marcy Gala-way." We stepped through the door and out onto the stage.

Nothing had prepared me for the shock of seeing all those people. There must have been two hundred of them assembled there on the rows of metal folding chairs. The room quivered with little coughs and stir-rings, with shifting feet and the sudden stunning flash of a camera.

In a daze I took my seat. I couldn't tear myself away from the crowd in front of me, some strangers, some people I had known all my life. Mom and Dad sat in the second row from the back; in all our years at Lake Marinac this was the first time they'd ever attended the *Scandals,* and they didn't want to be too conspicuous. And there was old Mr. Douglas, leaning forward expect-antly, cocking his better ear toward me.

Then for an instant my heart seemed to stop. Right in the second row sat a small dark woman with a fan-shaped comb in her shining black hair. Carmen Calderón.

"Go on," Liz whispered, nudging me back to reality. I became aware that long seconds had ticked by since we stepped out onto the stage.

Automatically my hands found the posi-tion they knew so well, and suddenly the opening notes flooded into the room.

Something had changed. The presence of

so many people in that small space absorbed the echoes which had grown so familiar in our nights of rehearsal. The notes of my guitar were softer, almost caressing, and though she stood right beside me, Liz's flute sounded smooth and tender and far away. In a rush I knew that the arching, twining harmonies we wove were exactly right.

It was over very quickly. We stood to a respectable round of applause. Liz offered a cool smile in return and made the slightest bow of acknowledgment. But I wore a very unprofessional ear-to-ear grin, and when Miss Calderón lifted her hand in salute, I almost knocked over Liz's music stand.

Backstage Roy threw his arms around both of us at once. "When do we hit Carnegie Hall?" He laughed. "I want to be your road manager."

"We did it!" I exclaimed. "I can't believe I didn't mess up or anything." I turned to Liz. "Hey, want to do an encore? That was fun."

"Aha, fame has already gone to your head," said Roy. "You'll be addicted to it in no time."

All Roy's attention was focused upon me, I realized. Liz slipped away to put her flute back into its case, but Roy's hand still rested on my shoulder. He still smiled at me with pride—and was there something else there too?

The back screen door swung open and

past Roy's shoulder I saw Brian burst in, his face split with his broadest, most lopsided grin. Then he stopped short. His grin vanished, and he stared at me and Roy with surprise and dismay.

"Brian," I called brightly, as Roy's hand fell to his side, "congratulations! You brought down the house. Where were you just now?"

For a moment he looked away, as though he wanted to hide the expression on his face. "I went and sat in the audience," he said in an odd, flat voice. "I wanted to hear you from out there."

I glanced at Roy apologetically and hurried over to Brian. "You did? It never occurred to me you'd go out there. I thought you'd be hanging out back here and I'd see you as soon as I got off." I was talking too fast, stringing words together just to fill up the silence.

"Maybe I should have," Brian said. "Maybe I made a mistake."

I wasn't sure what he meant by that. "That bad, huh?" I laughed. "You should have skipped the whole thing."

"Are you kidding?" Brian's grin revived a little. "I wouldn't have missed it for anything. I felt like telling everybody, 'Hey, I know her. She's been my best friend since fourth grade.'"

He put his hand on my arm and I followed him outside onto the gravel walk. It was intermission, and people from the audience milled around with members of the cast, smoking cigarettes, talking in little groups, exclaiming how good it was to breathe the cool fresh air. We stood beneath the spreading canopy of the oak tree and I fumbled for something to say. "Liz was the one who really carried it off," I told Brian. "We're going to get together again to play some more, just on our own."

My eyes strayed to the door and my ears strained for the sound of Roy's voice. I shouldn't have rushed away from him like that. What must he think of me after he'd been so friendly?

"Was that your guitar teacher?" Brian asked. "That exotic-looking lady in the front?"

"That was her, all right. I told her I was playing, but I never thought she'd really come."

There was still no sign of Roy, but suddenly Eilene broke away from a giggling group of girls and waved at us. "Hey, Marcy, Brian—there's a party after the show. Over at Roy's place. Everybody's invited."

"Great!" I called. "We'll be there."

But Brian was silent. He scuffed up a clump of weeds with the toe of his sneaker. "What's the matter?" I asked him. "Don't you want to go?"

"Oh, I don't know."

"What do you mean?"

"I'm just not in the mood, that's all. I know what it'll be like."

"Ah, come on," I exclaimed. "You had fun in the show. I thought you were getting over all that. You know—"

"Oh, I did enjoy doing the skit, more than I ever expected. Some of those people are really okay. But that's not it."

"Well, what's the matter, then?" I demanded. But before he could answer I went on, "Everybody'll want to see you there. You and your dad were the best part of the show, you know. Just go for a little while at least. We can go together, if that'll make you feel better."

"Oh, okay," he said. "I'll put in an appearance if you really want me to."

Intermission was almost over, and Mrs. Lowell hovered around, gesturing and pointing to urge the cast back inside. "We'll see you at the party," she said as we brushed past her through the screen door.

"Sure," I said, to cover Brian's silence. "We wouldn't miss it."

Back inside I began to relax. For me the show was all over except for the curtain call.

I walked over to Roy's house with Brian. I guess I was half afraid he'd never show up there at all if I let him out of my sight.

Even three houses away we heard the

sounds of the party—loud talk and laughter and the steady pulse of rock music kept to a moderate volume for the sake of all the adults present. Mrs. Lowell stood at the front door greeting each new guest with the graciousness of a queen at a court banquet. Beside her was a gray-haired man in a tweed suit who almost blended into the background. He had to be Roy's father, but it was hard to believe he could belong to the Lowell family.

"So good of you to come," Mrs. Lowell said warmly, pressing my hand. "Why don't you leave your guitar here on the porch? And, Brian, you stole the show. You and your father were wonderful."

Brian grinned at her. "We had a great time doing the skit. I might decide to become a poacher someday. It seems like fun."

I had never heard Brian say so much to Mrs. Lowell before. Maybe now that he was really at the party he had determined to make the best of it.

Where would I find Roy, I wondered. I felt like something had begun between us as he sat backstage holding my hand. Tonight, at this party, we would build on that beginning . . . .

But the first person we encountered as we crossed the porch into the living room was Carmen Calderón. She was already the center of an admiring circle, but she broke away when she caught sight of me, exclaiming, "Marcy, I have to congratulate you."

She threw her arms around me and stretched up on tiptoe to kiss me on each cheek. I smelled the heady fragrance of her perfume. "You made me proud of you tonight," she said. "All your hard work, it is beginning to—how do you say?—it begins to reward you."

I hardly knew what to say. In the past three years she had never bestowed such high praise upon me. "I wouldn't be anywhere without you," I said truthfully.

"Ah, yes, but the teacher can do nothing without good material to work with." But she held up her hand in warning. "I do not say you are ready for the concert stage. But for your first public appearance you have done very well."

Brian had joined his parents in a little crowd over by the windows. Mr. Townsend looked as though he wanted to fend off his enthusiastic admirers, but his wife's delighted smile seemed to take in the whole room. I would never have pictured the Townsends at a party with the Lowells, but here they were, and they were surviving very well.

I edged my way through the press of people to the refreshment table, two tables pulled together and draped with a flowered linen cloth. There were two bowls of punch and dish after dish of fancy hors d'oeuvres. I took a plate and selected an enticing variety of stuffed mushrooms, cheeses, and little puff pastries. I was about to ladle myself some punch when a voice at my back cautioned, "Watch out! That bowl's spiked, and you're a minor, you know."

"Oh, Roy!" I giggled. "Why'd you have to go and tell me?"

"Maybe I shouldn't have, come to think of it," Roy said. "Oh, well, too late now."

"These are delicious," I said, sampling one of the little pastries. It was filled with some kind of spiced meat. "How did your mom have time to put together this open house on top of all the work she was doing with the *Scandals*?"

"She finds the time," Roy said, shrugging. "Dad just puts up with it, but she loves to entertain people."

I ought to think of something a little more personal to say, something that would pull our conversation away from other people and back to us. But instead I heard myself say, "Well, she sure does it right—all this food, all these people."

"Hey, have you seen Kate?" Roy asked.

"Your sister? No, I didn't even know she was here."

"Yeah, she came up for the weekend. I've got to tell her something." But he made no move to go look for her. We munched hors d'oeuvres for a few moments in silence, and Roy began swaying to the music that thumped and rolled in the background.

"Too bad Mom made me promise not to turn it up any higher," he said, pointing to the stereo on a low table by the wall. "Hey, do you like to dance?"

"Sure," I said. It would be wonderful to dance with Roy, to have that living proof that to him I wasn't just one of the boys.

But instead of asking me, Roy brushed the subject aside and went on, "Sometime you ought to hear these speakers when I can really turn them up. They're fantastic —lift the roof right off the house."

Before I could answer him, Mom cried, "Oh, there you are!" I whirled to see her and Dad making their way toward me through the crowd.

"We looked around for you after the show," Dad said. "But we must have missed you somehow. So we figured you'd be over here."

"What did you think of the *Scandals*?" I asked.

"It had its moments," Mom admitted. "I don't know about that bit the Spaldings did, though. What was it she said when he wanted to commit suicide—she told him to do it beautifully?"

"But you were great," Dad said. "You made the show."

Roy tapped my shoulder. "I'll be seeing you," he said. "I've got to go find Kate."

"Sure," I said. I watched wistfully as he disappeared, and wondered how I would manage to start a fresh conversation with him all over again.

"We saw Miss Calderón," Dad was saying. "You know, she told us you should consider going to a conservatory of music after you graduate."

In an instant I forgot all about Roy. "She did? She never told me!"

"She will," Mom assured me. "She says you'll have to study piano in addition to your guitar, and get some more music theory, whatever that is. She'll explain it all to you at your lesson Thursday."

Dad gazed around the room. "You know, this is really a first," he said thoughtfully. "I can't remember ever seeing so many summer people and year-rounders collected together under one roof, can you, Martha?"

Mom shook her head. "I think you started the snowball rolling, Marcy," she said. "You offered to help with the show and then to play that piece, then the Townsends got involved, and then of course we all had to come to see you. . . ."

"That's right," said Roy's mother. I hadn't even noticed her come up beside us. "It's been terrific, watching everybody work together. In fact"—and she tossed Dad her most irresistible smile—"I think you ought to propose a toast."

"Me?" Dad exclaimed, and he actually blushed under his tan.

"Of course," said Mrs. Lowell. Dad stared at her in dismay as she stepped to the refreshment table and banged on the punch bowl to get the crowd's attention.

At last voices hushed and Roy even turned the music down to a whisper. "We're all here tonight because we've just put on a show I know I'll always remember," Mrs. Lowell began. "From what people have been telling me, it seems like this year's show has been something special. And here's the man who makes everything work at Lake Marinac—" There was a little ripple of appreciative laughter as she pointed at Dad, "Mr. Don Galaway, and he's going to propose a toast."

Dad looked from Mom to me for help, but neither of us had any idea what he ought to say. "I've always had a feeling about that woman," Mom said in a low voice. "She has a way of getting people to do whatever she wants."

Dad cleared his throat. "Well, believe it or not, we're all here together tonight," he began. Then I guess he decided he needed a different approach. For a moment he hesitated, gathering his thoughts. Then he proclaimed, "Tonight proves something I've always believed—that Lake Marinac is a unique place on the face of this earth. Anything can happen here. So"—raising his punch glass high—"here's to Lake Marinac."

"To Lake Marinac," came the scattered echoes all around the room. Plastic cups rose and suddenly everyone talked at once.

There was a burst of laughter from the kitchen, and Roy turned the music up to the approved pitch once more.

Apparently he hadn't found Kate, but he didn't seem very concerned. He stood near the stereo, bent in an avid conversation with Eilene. Her high clear laughter floated above the murmur of voices in the room, and as I watched, Roy put his hand on her shoulder and they began to dance.

They didn't have much space and they kept bumping into people, but that didn't seem to bother them. I couldn't tell what step they were doing, and whatever it was, they couldn't do it very well because of the crowd. But Eilene's hips wiggled and her red curls bounced, and she gazed up at Roy as if she were Cinderella and he were the prince.

Roy held both of her hands now, and he kept leaning down to whisper in her ear. Maybe it was just because he was so much taller than she was, but there was something about the way he did it that made me look away. But perhaps when this song ended it would be my turn. This party was going to be special for us, wasn't it—for Roy and me?

"Marcy, you were wonderful," exclaimed Mrs. Forbes of the post office. "I'm going to write my son, you know, the one in the navy—I'm going to write him that we'll be reading about you one of these days."

"Thanks. I don't know about that, though."

The song faded out, and in the little pool of quiet before the next one began I heard Roy say, ". . . at the drive-in tomorrow. You'll like it. I can get the car. . . ." Then the next song overtook him with a clattering piano, and they were dancing again.

Had I misunderstood the way he held my hand, the way he looked at me when I got off the stage? Roy had made me feel special, important to him, but now again it was Eilene he really cared about. Always Eilene . . .

I wandered out onto the porch where the music was muffled and I could escape Eilene's ringing laughter. There were fewer people out here. The air was hazy with the pungent smoke from Mr. Abano's pipe as he sat listening to Mr. Douglas. It was one of Mr. Douglas' stories of the blizzard of '47, which he said made the winter of '79 seem like a picnic.

And there was Kate Lowell on the love seat beside Brian's brother, Tom. One glance at Tom told me he had already fallen prey to her. Kate's voice was a confidential murmur, so low Tom had to bend close to catch her words. He gazed at her face as though she were the first girl he had ever seen.

It was the Lowell curse, I thought. They would captivate, they would enthrall, only to cast us aside. I had a wild impulse to warn Tom, to shout, "Be careful, keep away from her. She'll only make you miserable."

"You ready to go yet?"

"Brian!" I cried, and there was a little catch in my throat. "I didn't hear you come up."

"Well, are you ready, or do you want to hang around here some more yet?"

"Let's go now. I think I've had enough."

I remembered my manners long enough to thank Mrs. Lowell for the lovely evening. "You're not going so soon," she protested. "They're delivering pizzas in about fifteen minutes."

But Brian didn't give in to her. "No, we really have to go," he said, and he even remembered my guitar where I had stood it in the corner.

I breathed in the pure night air, scented with earth and honeysuckle. Katydids rasped back and forth from the trees, and from somewhere in the woods came the endless chant of a whippoorwill.

To my surprise Brian didn't turn toward my house, but began to walk along the beach instead. He knew me so well, I marveled. He was right, of course—what I needed was a good long walk to help me get my thoughts together.

Little waves lapped at the shore, and our feet left a deep trail in the damp sand. We were halfway down the beach when Brian finally broke the silence. "What did you think of the party?"

"Oh, it was great to see everybody there. But then, things kind of got to me." Usually I hated to admit that Brian was right and I was wrong, but now it didn't even seem to matter.

"Yeah, me too," Brian said. "It wasn't bad or anything—I just didn't really want to be there."

I had nothing to say to that. We went a few more steps in silence before Brian said, "You know, some of those people really are all right. Like that Liz—she's smart and interesting and not even stuck up. And Mrs. Lowell's okay in her way, I guess. But then some of the other ones . . ."

Here it comes, I thought. I didn't want to listen to an attack on Roy. I wanted to pretend that he didn't exist.

"Like that Eilene," I burst out. "That girl—she's like a little brook—she just babbles and chuckles along, she acts like there's nothing in her head. I don't understand what makes her so interesting to people, except she's little and pretty."

"Interesting to who?" Brian demanded. "She sure doesn't do much for me. Maybe Roy sees something in her, but it beats me what."

There was his name. He did exist, I couldn't deny it. "She's been to all these places, she's got this good education, but she doesn't show it off," I said, trying to make some sense out of it. "She just kind of bounces along on the surface of things. Maybe that's what guys really want."

"Not *all* guys," Brian said. "If you ask me, I think she's boring as heck."

"Oh, I don't mean you," I said. "You're different. But what do other guys—"

"You mean Roy Lowell, don't you?" To my surprise, there was no bitterness in his voice. It was just a simple question.

"Well, okay, guys like Roy Lowell—what do *they* want in a girl?"

Brian considered. "I think what he— what guys like him want is to be light about everything. They don't want to get serious about girls, about anything. They're just looking to have a good time."

Maybe Brian was right. Perhaps that had been my fatal mistake. I had encouraged Roy to talk about serious things that afternoon when we painted the furniture—no wonder he had been so pleased when Eilene turned up. And he had seen how serious I felt about playing the guitar, too. Sure, who would want to go out with a girl who might start talking about Andrés Segovia?

Could I ever learn to be light and laughing like Eilene? Could I bounce the conversation back and forth like a Ping-Pong ball, never letting it touch the ground?

"Maybe there's still hope for me," I sighed. "Maybe someday I'll learn."

Suddenly Brian stopped. He put his hand on my shoulder and swung me to face him. "Please don't," he said softly. "I like you just the way you are."

I laughed and gave him a big hug. "I don't know about that," I said, "but thanks anyway. You know, you're the best best friend I could ever have."

9

Wow, I could play all afternoon," I sighed as Liz and I brought the little Dowland air to a lilting close. "You sure you want to go for a swim?"

Liz laughed as she put her flute back into its case. "We can play some more, you know. I'll be here two and a half weeks yet."

"You just can't imagine," I said slowly, "how great it is to be able to play with—with a real musician. I mean, you're probably so used to it after Interlocken and everything."

"That's why it's so much fun to play with you," Liz said. "You're really enthusiastic, you don't take anything for granted."

"Want to play again tomorrow?" I cast a longing glance at the mound of sheet music piled on my bed.

"Sure, right after lunch again," Liz promised. "Come on—get your bathing suit on, let's go."

"You want to come swim off our dock?" I asked as I dug my yellow two-piece out of my bottom drawer.

"Oh, let's go over to the beach. Some of the other kids might be hanging out there."

I hesitated, the top of my suit dangling from my hand by one shoulder strap. Did I really want to run into Eilene and Roy? Was I ready for that this afternoon?

"Which other kids?" I asked her.

"Oh, you know—Carla and Eilene, maybe Bob Hansen. Roy had to go some place this afternoon, or else they'd probably be out water-skiing."

"Oh, okay," I decided. "Sure—let's go to the beach." As long as Roy wouldn't be there, I told myself, it wouldn't be too bad. And if I was ever going to learn Eilene's secret, I needed to get to know her better.

"Hey, you guys, over here," Eilene called, catching sight of us as we padded across the sand.

She and Carla had staked out a claim near the swings, a little homestead of beach towels, woven straw bags, tubes of suntan lotion, a transistor radio and Carla's inevitable hoard of food.

"Hi," I said shyly as we spread out our towels beside theirs and settled down.

"Hurry up and eat a couple of those Milky

Ways," Eilene said, pointing to a paper bag on the corner of Carla's pink towel. "If you don't eat them, I'm afraid I'll get tempted."

"You don't need to watch your weight, Eilene," Carla pointed out as Liz and I helped ourselves. "I'm the one who's dieting all the time." She stuffed an empty candy wrapper back into the bag and pulled out a package of Life Savers.

"You're not dieting today, are you?" Liz asked.

"Well, no, but I did yesterday. Me and Bob drove down the hill, and I didn't have a shake with my hamburger."

I was grateful that I'd never had to worry about gaining weight. I'd always been able to eat anything I wanted and I never grew any wider—only taller and taller.

I stretched out on my stomach, propped myself up on my elbows and observed Eilene. She had a soft, golden tan by now, the kind you see on posters advertising vacations in Bermuda. She lay sprawled on her towel sifting sand between her fingers, watching three little girls as they argued who would get the swing without a broken seat. After a while she picked up a stick and began to draw idly in the sand. She hardly looked down at what she was doing. "So, you and Bob are going together these days?" she asked Carla.

Carla yawned. "Oh, I don't know. He's okay, I guess, but he never *says* anything. I don't know if I like him all that much."

"You never give anybody a chance, that's your trouble," said Eilene. "Oh, hey, turn that song up—I love it."

Carla turned up the radio. It was a slow gentle song sung by two women's voices. I'd always thought it was kind of pretty, but now I really listened for the first time. Maybe the words or the smooth flow of the melody would tell me something about who Eilene really was.

"You're awfully quiet, Marcy," said Liz. "What are you thinking about?"

All of a sudden a line popped into my head, something Brian had said once in the school cafeteria when somebody commented that he was too quiet. "Oh," I said airily, "I'm busy taking notes for my novel."

For a second they all stared at me, and Eilene's eyes grew very round with amazement. Then they were all laughing.

"Am I in it?" asked Eilene. "I want a big part."

"Me too," Carla added. "I want to be the romantic lead."

"Okay," I told her. "You're being held hostage in the castle till the hero comes to rescue you."

"Hey, great." Carla giggled. "That's the only way you'll ever keep me away from Pizza Hut and McDonald's."

Maybe they really weren't so different from the girls at Callonville Regional, I thought in wonder. It was hard to remember now that Liz had given her first recital

when she was nine, or that Eilene gave
Spain a low rating compared to all the other
countries she had visited. As we lay there
on the sand, I felt only how much alike we
all really were.

"Well, I'm ready for a swim," Liz announced. "I'm going to melt out here in
another minute."

"I'm coming too," I told her. I kicked off
my sandals and got to my feet. As I passed
Eilene, I paused to see what she had been
drawing in the sand with her little stick.

Along the edge of her towel stood a line of
tiny dancers. Some had their hands joined,
others bowed, a few stretched upward.
They were only simple figures, just lines
cut into the sand. But each one was a little
different.

Eilene saw me gazing down at them and
flushed. She tried to cover her work with
her outspread hands.

"Hey, that's neat," I exclaimed. "I didn't
know you could draw—besides doing posters, I mean."

Liz bent to get a better look, and even
Carla glanced over lazily from her towel to
see what was going on.

"Oh, I'm not any good at it," Eilene said.
"I'm just doodling." With a swish of her
stick the little people disappeared as if she
had waved a magic wand.

"Why'd you do that?" Liz protested. "I
hardly got a chance to see."

"You didn't miss a thing," Eilene said.

"Go ahead, try the water—it's freezing, though."

The sand burned the soles of my feet as we raced down to the shore. At the first touch of the water my feet tingled with relief. But as we splashed farther and farther out, the water seemed to grow steadily colder until my body argued at every step. For a few moments I paused, the water up to my hips, and my toes burrowed into the soft sandy bottom.

"I'm not so sure I want to get wet after all," Liz said beside me.

"You've just got to make up your mind and do it," I told her from long years of experience. "Like this."

I poised on my toes for an instant and let myself fall forward. In the first moment the shock of the cold took my breath away. Then I began to swim with long smooth strokes. A splash and a cry behind me told me that Liz, too, had finally taken the plunge.

"Want to swim out to the ski raft?" Liz called.

"Okay, come on," I said. I broke into the breaststroke, which was always more relaxing to me than the crawl, and headed for the bobbing green raft that was anchored some hundred yards offshore.

It wasn't long before I realized that Liz wasn't a strong swimmer. I slowed down so I wouldn't outdistance her and watched anxiously as her strokes became more and more choppy with tiredness. Halfway to the raft she stopped and began to tread water, only her wet brown head swaying above the surface.

"I don't know if I'm going to make it," she gasped. "Maybe we ought to head back."

"It's just as far to go back as it is to get there," I pointed out. "Anyway, the sandbar's just a little farther. It's shallow enough to stand by the raft, don't forget."

Liz rested a little longer. Then she rolled over and began a determined sidestroke that carried her to the sandbar. In another few moments we clambered up onto the ski raft and flopped onto the sun-warmed planks.

"I sure must be out of shape," Liz sighed. "You'd think after all summer here I could swim that little way without conking out, wouldn't you?"

"You did okay," I tried to assure her. "You made it, right?"

"I'll never be as good as you are," she said. "Do you ever swim in meets, for a team or anything?"

I was startled by the admiration in her voice. "No, for me it's always just been something to do for fun. I don't have any discipline about it."

A cloud drifted past the sun and the air grew suddenly chilly. I hugged my knees and looked back to the beach, where I could just make out Eilene and the others sprawled on the sand. I wondered if Liz was ready to head back yet.

"Are you going to the big dance?" she asked me suddenly.

"What big dance?"

"Didn't you hear about it? I saw a poster this morning at the community house. It's Labor Day weekend. Friday night the parents are having one for themselves, with one of those old-fashioned Glenn Miller-type bands. And then Saturday night there's a dance for us with a live group from the city. Somebody told me they're friends of Roy's."

"Oh," I said. Suddenly my mind was racing, but I tried to keep the excitement out of my voice as I asked, "Are you going?"

Liz hesitated. "Oh, I don't know. Jack, my boyfriend from down home, he wouldn't mind. But I might feel funny there without a date. What about you?"

A year ago I would never have considered attending a dance at the community house. But now things were different. I knew better than to dream that Roy might ask me, though. It was ridiculous to think of such a thing. Still, it would be wonderful . . . . If we could go together, dance and talk through the long evening, I would know that this summer had truly changed my life.

"I probably won't go either," I told Liz. "Unless—"

"Unless what?"

"Oh, nothing. Do you think Carla will go? Or Eilene?"

"Probably." The sun emerged again and we stretched out to take full advantage of it. "Poor Eilene," Liz sighed. "She's so afraid to let anybody know she has a brain in her head."

"What do you mean?" I asked with interest.

"Oh, you know—like the way she got so funny about those little pictures in the sand. She's got to be pretty smart if she got into Hawkins, but I think she's scared people won't like her if they find out— especially boys."

I remembered how Eilene had giggled and gotten so confused when she was explaining about the raffle to decide who would water-ski first. And I thought of how helpless she'd been that afternoon when we painted furniture with Roy. Was it really all just an act?

"Maybe she's right," I said. "I don't think boys—well, a lot of boys—do like girls to be too smart, do you?"

Liz propped herself up on her elbows and looked at me hard. "Well, maybe some of them are like that, like Roy or Bob. But Jack's not that way, and I don't think your friend Brian is either."

"So if Eilene wants a guy like Roy, she's smart enough to play dumb," I said. "I guess that's what you've got to do."

"Sure, if you want somebody like that," Liz said. "I don't think it's worth it myself. What's so great about somebody who makes you put yourself down like that?"

It was a good question, one I couldn't answer. But there was something about Roy that made girls feel he was worth any sacrifice.

After a while the sun drove us back into the water again. Liz switched strokes two or three times, but she made it all the way to the beach without stopping to rest. She grinned with satisfaction as we splashed ashore.

Carla sat up and handed me my towel. "You guys are more ambitious than I am," she said. "I get worn out just swimming in the bathtub."

I dug a comb out of my bag and began to work the tangles out of my hair. Two little boys dashed for the swings, kicking a cloud of sand at us as they passed.

Carla turned to Eilene and picked up the conversation that had broken off when we arrived. "Well, I never heard of Stevie and the Angels. I don't see what's such a big deal."

"Roy says they're fantastic," Eilene said. "They played all July at this club called the Last Ditch."

So she had already talked to Roy about the band, the dance. He must have invited her, then. Slowly, methodically, my fingers went on working the knots out of my hair.

"I never heard of the Last Ditch, either," Carla said. "It can't be much."

"It gets me sometimes the way Roy plays games," Eilene said, studying her nails. "Like we had this really long talk about the band. Then he didn't even ask me to the dance. He just kind of acted like, 'Well, I haven't made up my mind who I want to go with, I have so many to choose from, you know.' "

My hands shook a little and I had to look away, over to the kids on the swings, so no one would guess how important Eilene's words were to me. Liz had to be right—what was so great about a guy who didn't want you to reveal that you were a reasonably intelligent person? But Roy was Roy. There was something about him I couldn't resist, and if he still hadn't invited Eilene to the dance, that meant I had a fighting chance.

10

Every morning I awoke with the thought that today might be *the* day, the day I could hear from Roy. But life went along as usual and there wasn't a thing I could do about it. Mornings I helped out at the store. I smiled at customers and glanced up hopefully every time the screen door opened, only to see Mrs. Forbes or Mr. Flannery or the Murphy twins. The afternoons were my own, for swimming or reading or practicing the guitar. Liz and I got together a couple more times to play duets, but this week she had gone down to the city to do something with her boyfriend and his family. Brian was working extra time to fill in for Dolly, who'd gotten food poisoning ("Not from any of our hamburgers, of course," he insisted), so I didn't see much of him, either. The way things were going, it looked as though we'd never find time to climb up to the lookout this summer.

Day by day summer slipped away, and Labor Day weekend crept closer and closer. Only six more days until the dance, I thought as I headed home for lunch that Monday. By now Roy must have made up his mind whom to invite—and obviously it wasn't me. Maybe I'd go to the beach and look for Eilene this afternoon, see what I could find out. But did I really want to know?

Mom was out, but she had already picked up the mail and there was a letter for me on the kitchen table. It was from Kathy in Maine. I tore it open and counted the pages —five! I'd read it slowly, stretch out the pleasure of it as long as I could over lunch.

Then I spotted the note, just a little slip of paper with a few words in Mom's neat script. "Gone shopping. Cold chicken in the fridge." And "P.S. A boy called. He'll call back."

No name, just "a boy called." That meant it couldn't be Brian. He worked today, for one thing, and besides, Mom had known his voice for years. This had to be someone else, someone she didn't recognize.

I found the cold chicken, a couple of deviled eggs and some potato salad. I switched on the radio for company and settled down with my lunch and Kathy's letter. But I kept glancing back at the note propped against the sugar bowl. "A boy called. He'll call back."

I thought over the boys I knew from school. It could be Peter Jaworski—he called once back in May to ask me out to a movie. Or it might be Dan Holloway. He called up once in a while just to talk, even though he never had much to say. If only he'd said what his name was! If only Mom had thought to ask him!

"Dear Marcy," Kathy wrote. "Hi. Sorry I took so long to write back. Well, to answer your questions: yes, they go out lobstering here, and I already went twice, but you've got to get up so *early*. . . ."

Sure, probably it was just Dan. I'd start dreaming about someone mysterious and exciting and it would turn out to be good old Dan Holloway. He'd talk around in a circle for ten minutes as if he were trying to get up the nerve to ask me out, and then instead he'd just say, "Well, I've gotta go now—'bye."

Suppose I waited all afternoon, guessing and wondering, and he just never called back! That would be so much worse than finding out it was only Dan Holloway— never finding out at all!

"How are things going with Roy?" Kathy asked in her letter. "He sounds like the kind that's too good-looking for his own good, if you know what I mean. Like that guy that was in my history class last year. . . ."

I finished the letter over a slice of peach pie and had just started the dishes when the phone rang. A plate slithered out of my soapy fingers and splashed into the dishpan. I crossed the room in two bounds and froze in front of the phone. I'd have to let it ring at least twice more. It took supreme willpower, but I stood perfectly still and counted one, two, even three more rings before I lifted the receiver from the wall and said, "Hello?"

"Hello," said a woman's voice. "Mary Sue?"

"No." My voice was flat. "I think you've got the wrong number."

"Oh, I'm sorry," the woman said. "I must have written it down wrong—oh, *honestly* . . ." She hung up, muttering to herself.

That would teach me a lesson, I told myself. I wouldn't think about this unknown boy anymore. I finished the dishes and went into my room to get my guitar. I took it out onto the front porch, sat on the swing and played through the Sor waltz. It really flowed now. I felt as though it truly belonged to me.

My hands rested on the strings as I remembered with a warm glow what Carmen Calderón had said after my lesson last week. "In order to study at a school of music after you graduate, you will need to begin your preparations now." Even though Dad and Mom had warned me that

Carmen had spoken to them the night of the *Scandals*, I was still overwhelmed. If Carmen said I should go on with my studies, that meant I was no longer just playing the guitar as a hobby. There was hope that I might become a serious musician someday.

Probably Liz had thought of herself that way most of her life, but for me it was a revelation. I'd always expected to graduate from high school and attend the community college in Callonville. Maybe I'd finish up at State if I could save the money. But now Carmen said she would recommend me for acceptance at the conservatory in New York where she had taught for three years, and maybe I could even win a scholarship. That meant that in two more years I might be able to leave home and launch out into a world of music and culture and stimulating new people.

A boy called . . . he'll call back. . . .

Well, if I wanted to get into the conservatory I couldn't sit around daydreaming. I ran through my fingering exercises and practiced some of the more difficult chord changes I would need for the new Villalobos piece Carmen had given me. I was just experimenting with the opening measures when the telephone rang again.

No real professional would jump up every time the phone rang. But I wasn't a real professional yet. I set the guitar down on the swing and dashed into the kitchen.

"Hello?" I said, and waited for the woman to ask for Mary Sue again.

"Hello, Marcy?"

But it was a boy's voice, and it wasn't Dan Holloway. It was—but I hadn't dared to think about it, it couldn't be. . . .

"Hey, Marcy, this is Roy."

"Oh, hi, Roy, how are you?" I tried to sound a little like Eilene, offhand, with the hint of a laugh welling up in my voice.

"Oh, pretty good. What about you? What have you been up to?"

"Just the usual. Helping out in the store, stuff like that." Couldn't I think of something more witty than that to say? I was beginning to sound like me again.

"Hey, I was thinking," Roy said, "you doing anything Saturday night?"

Saturday night. That couldn't be—but it was—and the receiver began to shake in my hand. "You mean Saturday of Labor Day weekend? No, no—nothing."

"Fantastic. You want to go to the dance?"

Probably that stunned silence lasted only one or two seconds. Thoughts tumbled through my head so fast I don't even remember what they were. But finally I heard myself saying, "Oh, sure, I'd love it," and I didn't sound like Eilene at all by then. I was no one but myself, all eagerness, waiting at Roy's beck and call.

"Fantastic," Roy said. "Hey, I got this really neat band to come up. You've got to hear them."

"I know. Stevie and the Angels," I said. I felt a little light-headed.

"Beautiful! You've already heard of them," Roy exclaimed. "They're starting to get big. So I'll see you Saturday, then— around eight."

"Yeah, around eight," I repeated, as if I were in a daze. He hadn't asked Eilene, he'd asked me! At the biggest event of the summer he wanted to be with me!

"Anyway," Roy was saying, "I'll see you between now and then. We can work out the details."

"Sure, I'll see you around."

"Fantastic," Roy said again, and "'bye."

"'Bye," I echoed, and I held the dead receiver in my hand.

I went back out onto the porch and sat on the swing. For a while I couldn't believe it had really happened. I'd always imagined that I'd be elated if Roy ever called me up and asked me for a real date. But now, as the reality of it slowly sank in, I felt overwhelmed, almost scared, instead. This was what I'd been dreaming of for so long, my big chance to show him I could be just as lively and carefree and fun to be with as Eilene or anybody else. But what if I froze up and couldn't think of a thing to say? What if I stumbled over my own feet trying to dance and turned the whole evening into a disaster?

I wouldn't let that happen, I promised myself. How could I be so pessimistic? Roy had called me, we were going to the dance together, and it was going to be a truly unforgettable evening. When Roy and the rest of the summer people were gone, and Lake Marinac was snowed in for another long lonely winter, I would have this time with Roy to remember and relive again and again.

We were finishing dinner that night when Brian's bicycle bell rang outside and he called, "Come on, let's go down the hill for ice cream."

I glanced at Mom and she nodded, giving me a reprieve from washing the dishes. In another moment I was out through the back door and wheeling my bike out of the garage. Our bells exchanged cheerful greetings and we were off.

I would have to tell Brian that I was going to the dance with Roy. He had mellowed since the *Scandals* and maybe by now he'd understand and wouldn't try to argue with me. Still I was in no hurry to bring up the subject.

The wind brushed my face as we started down the first gentle incline that led to Marinac Hill. Then, as the hill grew steeper, my hair whipped back and I felt the thrill of surging speed. Ahead of me Brian began to sing. It was a song we'd learned at school back in fifth grade: "Speed bonnie boat like a bird on the wing, Onward, the sailors cry . . ."

"Carry the lad who was born to be king, Over the sea to Skye." My own voice lifted with the familiar words, with the melody that rose and fell like waves and carried us, faster and faster, down the hill in a long, glorious sweep.

I applied the brakes as we neared the bottom, where Marinac Road met the highway in Callonville. "I ought to do that more often," I said as we drew to a stop in front of Baskin-Robbins.

"I get to do it every morning on my way to work," Brian said. "It's a great way to start the day—before I start ladling out cole slaw."

"But then you've got the trip home," I said. "That's a sobering thought."

Baskin-Robbins wasn't too crowded yet. More kids would probably come in later when the drive-in let out. Brian ordered a double German chocolate cake, and after a lot of thought I chose a cone with one scoop butter brickle and one of Swiss chocolate almond. Brian brought two glasses of water and we settled down at a table in the corner.

Now was my chance to tell him about the dance. But I licked my ice cream in silence.

Brian dug into his German chocolate cake with gusto. "My poor brother," he said after a couple of spoonfuls. "He's really hung up on that Kate Lowell."

Could he read my mind? Did he know

that Roy Lowell was in my thoughts that very minute?

"I thought so," I said casually. "I saw it all starting up at that party."

"He's hitchhiking down to the city to see her this weekend," Brian said. "Mom and Dad think he's nuts, but he's got this idea she'll be impressed by the hardships he goes through for her."

If I didn't tell him myself, he was sure to hear it from somebody else, and then he'd want to know why I hadn't mentioned it. . . .

"Do you think she will be?" I asked. "Impressed, I mean?"

Brian shrugged. "Oh, maybe at first she'll think it's neat. But she'll get restless —she's the type."

I turned my ice-cream cone. "How do you know?"

"She's probably just like Roy." He paused for a moment before he went on, "Hey, by the way—about that dance Saturday night . . ."

It was too late. I couldn't tell him myself. We really did live in a small town—he must have heard from somebody else already. In another second he'd launch into all his old warnings and objections, and tell me he'd always thought I had better sense.

So I plunged in before he had a chance to begin. "I know what you're going to say, but look at it from my point of view. How often do I ever get to go to something like that? I hadn't really expected to go, but then when I got the chance . . ."

I trailed off. Brian stared at me, his spoon poised in midair. "What do you mean—when you got the chance?"

Suddenly it had all grown very confusing. "With Roy," I stammered. "I mean—when Roy asked me."

"Roy asked you?" Brian exclaimed. "When?"

"Today. This afternoon. But I thought you already knew, or guessed, or something."

"So what did you tell him?" Brian demanded. "You're not going to go with him, are you?"

"Of course I am," I cried. "Why shouldn't I?"

"Because—well, because . . ." Brian's voice dropped with something like resignation. "Oh, what's the use? It's too late now."

"I don't see why you should get so upset about it," I told him. "We all had a good time working on the *Scandals,* you said yourself—"

"Is it true or is it not true," Brian broke in, "that you were kind of disgusted when we left that party? I thought you'd had enough of Roy for a while."

"That was different. Now that he called me up and asked me—well, it's just different, that's all."

Something cold and sticky trickled across

the back of my hand—my ice cream was melting. I licked around the rim of my cone, but I seemed to have lost my taste for Swiss chocolate almond.

"Well, it's all settled," said Brian. "Let's change the subject. Hey, I just read how they're diving for this sunken ship off Cape Cod."

"Brian, come on," I pleaded. "Maybe you can't understand because you're not a girl. It's just that I've got this opportunity and—"

"And you can't turn it down," he finished for me. "No, I can understand that. You better go with him, if that's how you feel about it. I hope you have a good time."

Why should it matter so much to Brian anyway? I wondered. Listening to him, I could almost think that he wanted to ask me to the dance himself and that he was jealous of Roy. But that wouldn't make any sense. Brian and I were friends. No matter who either of us went out with, nothing would ever change that.

"Well, I guess we better head out," Brian said after a while. "Sometimes that trek up the hill seems like a journey without end—a quest for the Holy Grail or something."

I tried to laugh and just about succeeded. But our trip home had lost the zest of the ride down the hill to Baskin-Robbins—and it wasn't only because now we were pumping our way back uphill.

11

I don't understand why you're so nervous," Mom said as I jumped up from the swing to pace across the porch again. "You weren't even this bad when you played in the *Scandals*."

"This is different," I said, but I could hardly explain it even to myself. I knew I looked my best in my new pink dress. It had taken a lot of hard talking to persuade Mom that the dress was a necessity—sleeveless, with a deep scoop neck, it was a filmy chiffon that swirled and floated as I walked.

But could I handle myself properly among the summer kids? Suppose I seemed too shy and awkward, or too serious—or too tall—Roy might be sorry that he invited me after all.

"You know," Mom said, "I was saying to your father last night, maybe we should have gone to that dance they had last night with the big band—the Van Horns went, so we wouldn't have been the only year-rounders there."

"Things sure are changing around here," I said. "A couple of months ago you would never have even thought of it."

"Oh, I don't know." Mom leafed through a magazine. "Now that you've sort of broken the ice, I figure maybe we ought to take advantage of things that are going on."

I stared out through the screen door, but no tall slim figure strode toward me along Lakefront Road. It was five minutes to eight, he wasn't even late yet. But what if I waited here on the porch and watched the sun set and saw all of the other couples pass on their way over to the community house and Roy never appeared?

I paced back to the swing and picked up a copy of the *Oracle*. There was an article about banning outboards of more than forty horsepower from the lake. And Dr. and Mrs. Hansen had celebrated their twenty-fifth anniversary. They smiled toothily at each other in the photograph, and Mrs. Hansen's hair was, as always, practically standing on end.

A step outside, two firm knocks on the screen door—and the paper dropped to the floor. But somehow I managed to rise slowly, to smooth my dress, to cross the room and open the door with a casual, "Oh, hi, Roy. Gee, I didn't expect you this soon."

Mom retreated discreetly into the living room, but not before she threw me a swift, knowing wink. Maybe I could convince Roy that I was superbly calm and collected, but Mom knew it was all a big front.

"I said eight o'clock," Roy pointed out. "I'm a man of my word." He paused to study me, and to my delight his eyes widened. "Hey," he said. "You really look great."

"Thanks," I said, flushing with pleasure. "You do, too." Were you supposed to say that to a boy? I wondered. But Roy did look almost dashing in gray trousers and a blue blazer, not quite formal, but not really casual either.

"Well, you ready?" he asked. He still stood on the top step.

Probably someone really experienced and sophisticated would have coyly kept him waiting. But I couldn't wait to get the adventure of the evening under way. "Sure," I answered. "Let's go."

"Stevie and the Angels got in this afternoon," Roy told me as we swung along down the road. "They'll be camping out in their van in front of our house tonight."

"I wonder what the neighbors will say to that," I said. "In conservative Lake Marinac."

A couple walked ahead of us, and I recognized Carla and Bob Hansen. So she had decided to go with him after all. Would Eilene be coming tonight? I wondered. I couldn't think who she would come with now that I was with Roy, but I couldn't picture her missing a big dance like this, either. Why had Roy chosen me instead of Eilene? Could he have begun to regret his decision?

But when I turned and met his gaze, he smiled at me as though I were someone very special. Beside him, I was no longer a gawky giraffe. I felt a quiet new assurance, as though I were older, ready to cope with anything that might come my way.

We caught up with Bob and Carla on the wooden porch of the community house. Through the open door drifted a hum of voices, and there was the jarring buzz of an amplifier.

For a few moments Bob and Roy talked about the band and when they had heard them last, at some place called the Yellow Submarine.

"I like your earrings," I told Carla, pointing to the fine silver hoops that swung from her ears.

"They're from Mexico," she said offhandedly. "My brother was down there, so he sent them for my birthday."

"Oh, that's interesting," I said. A few weeks ago I would have been awed by the idea that her brother was traveling to such a faraway place. But now I had the sudden thought that, if I could think of going to the conservatory, why couldn't I travel someday, too? Anything was possible.

"We may as well go in," Roy said. The community house was already crowded. I'd never realized there were so many kids my age at Lake Marinac this summer. There were even some here who I'd never seen before. But there wasn't a sign of Eilene. The room was decorated with Japanese lanterns and crepe-paper streamers, but the most startling thing of all was the band.

Stevie and the Angels had set up their equipment on the stage where Liz and I had performed our Bach prelude. They had an array of amplifiers and speakers, an organ, a set of drums, a bass and an electric guitar. Strobe lights flashed, and cords zigzagged everywhere. Four shaggy boys scrambled to and fro, arranging and rearranging.

"Come on," Roy said, gesturing toward the stage. "I want to introduce you."

We mounted the three steps and Roy called, "Hey, Stevie, come here and meet Marcy. She's kind of a musician too, she plays acoustic guitar."

"Far out," said Stevie, thrusting out a broad, powerful hand. His thick dark-brown hair was tied back with a piece of red yarn. His three companions were just as hairy as he was, and I reflected that they looked more like trolls than angels.

"This place is all right, you know," Stevie told Roy. "I can get into it here. Like the people seem really mellow."

"Yeah, I can dig what you're saying,"

answered Roy. "You ready to go on pretty soon? We can use some sound around here."

I'd never heard Roy talk like that before, using all that hip musician's jargon. He just slipped into it because he was with Stevie—and something about it seemed odd to me, almost artificial.

"Okay, just be cool," said Stevie. "Give us another minute. We've got to hook up Louie's amp."

We got off the stage and wandered over to the refreshment table at the far side of the room. There I discovered Liz setting out stacks of napkins and paper plates.

"Hi," I said. "I thought you said you weren't coming tonight."

"I guess I couldn't resist," she said. "Even though I haven't got a date, I figure I can help out here and maybe get to dance once in a while."

She glanced over at the stage and made a funny grimace. "Can you believe it? We're going from Bach to rock."

Roy offered me some potato chips and took a generous handful for himself. Suddenly a peal of guitar chords ripped over the murmur of voices in the room, and Stevie's voice crackled through the microphone to announce, "Hello, all you good people out there, we love you. We just want you to have a good time tonight, and this is just the beginning."

With a flourish they launched into their first number. Without a word Roy seized my hand and we swept out onto the dance floor.

There was something smooth and easy in all his movements, and as we danced, I felt I moved with a grace I'd never hoped to possess before. Was it only because Roy was my partner? Without him, would I turn back into Marcy the lanky tomboy, always stumbling over my own feet?

But if I were just a clumsy tomboy I wouldn't be here in the first place, would I? For a fleeting moment I remembered Roy's sister, Kate. She was as tall as I was, but still she was stunningly attractive. Well, I'd probably never be another Kate Lowell, but suddenly I knew that I was pretty in my own way.

"Okay, everybody," Stevie called at the close of the first song. "Here comes a little fast disco to loosen you all up. Get ready, get set, *go!*"

The band broke into a pulsing disco number with a driving relentless beat. I'd been impressed by Roy's dancing before, but now he really came to life. After a while Bob and Carla came to dance beside us, and then we were joined by two more couples, then a third. Before I realized how it happened we had formed a twisting shifting chain that wound and looped over the dance floor.

The music urged us on, faster and faster. The room faded, there was nothing but the pounding beat and our swaying, whirling bodies. I lost track of Roy; a strange boy in a red shirt led me through a dizzying turn. I had never known I could dance like this, but now I was drawn along like a chip of driftwood in a whirlpool.

One piece flowed into another until I had forgotten the beginning and couldn't imagine an end. And then suddenly I caught sight of Roy again. He was dancing with Carla.

They had drawn a little apart from the rest of us, a link broken from the end of the chain. For once Carla looked wide awake. Her cheeks glowed and her silver earrings bounced and swung. Roy danced as expertly as ever, and with Roy as her partner, even Carla seemed light on her feet.

But what jolted me was the look Roy gave her, a shining embracing smile as though she were the most special girl in his world. I'd seen that look on his face before. I had tried to believe it was reserved for me alone.

For the first time I was aware of my arms and legs. I commanded them through the motions of the dance, but they obeyed mechanically, alien to the rhythm. The boy in the red shirt eyed me with surprise and danced away to find a new partner.

Roy and Carla danced on as though no one else existed, and I ached inside as I watched them. I knew Carla wasn't any prettier or more interesting than I was, so why did Roy prefer to be with her now? Why did he look at her as if she were the one and only?

Maybe it didn't matter to Roy who he was with. Maybe he treated all girls to the same enchanting smile and light flirtatious banter. Maybe deep down none of it meant anything to him at all.

I remembered how close I'd felt to Roy that afternoon we painted furniture, and how easily he had turned from me to Eilene the moment she appeared. But how had Eilene felt when she saw me and Roy together in the stern seat of the outboard as she skied behind us, or when Roy held my hand backstage before my performance in the *Scandals*?

Brian had always said Roy was just out to have a good time, that he didn't want to get serious about anything or anybody. Brian had seen it all so clearly from the beginning. Why hadn't I listened to him? By now he must have decided I was a hopeless idiot. Suddenly I longed to see him again, to try to regain the respect I must have thrown away this summer.

At long last the music wound to a halt. As though he'd never been gone, Roy appeared beside me, grinning and perspiring. "Wow!" he exclaimed. "That was a happening, wasn't it?"

"It was a happening all right," I said.

He squeezed my shoulder. "Hey, Marcy, I knew you could water-ski, but you never told me you could dance like that."

"I never knew myself." Could I have been wrong after all? Maybe there was something the matter with me, maybe I was just jealous and possessive. Roy gave me an affectionate nudge toward the refreshment table. He was my partner for the evening, smiling, attentive, doing his best to make me feel appreciated. . . .

"Want some punch?" Roy asked. In the lull between songs his voice rang loud and clear.

"Okay."

He waved to Liz, still at work behind the table. "Two cups of punch," he called.

"Comin' up," Liz said, dipping in with the ladle.

"Hey, you're working too hard, Liz," Roy said. "Come on out and stretch your legs a little." He winked at her. "You can dance, I heard it through the grapevine."

Liz looked away. "Later maybe," she said. Maybe she already knew that wink could have been meant for anyone, for her or Carla, Eilene or me.

The music started up again. Roy shouted something to me, but I could hardly hear him over the blaring of the organ. From the way he pointed to the door, though, I understood that he wanted to go outside.

I hesitated. I didn't want to be alone with

Roy now—we had nothing to say to each other. But I couldn't think of any excuse to stay inside. Reluctantly I followed him out onto the wooden porch.

The air was cool and fresh, and it was a relief to get away from the pounding music and the press of people. "You having a good time, Marci-oh?" Roy asked, leaning against the railing.

"Sure, great." It was what he expected me to say. I kept my thoughts to myself.

"And the band? How do you like Stevie and the Angels?"

"Oh, they're fantastic." I had thought so, too, when I was caught up in the blaze of music and dancing. But now the whole evening seemed fuzzy and out of focus.

Roy edged closer to me along the railing. "We're leaving on Monday, you know," he said. "Monday Labor Day—that's the day after tomorrow."

I'd known it all summer. Day by day I'd ached with the knowledge that my opportunities to see him, to be with him, were dwindling, vanishing away. But now I only asked, "Will you be back next summer?"

"Maybe," he said. I'd never before heard the soft tender note that crept into his voice as he went on, "But that's such a long time—not to see you."

He was right beside me now. I glanced up at the overhead light and watched a brown moth flutter in circles against the bulb. I still held a paper cup of punch, but Roy's hand folded over my free hand as he asked, "Are you going to miss me?"

"I guess so—sure." Would he ask the same question of Eilene or Carla?

"You *guess* so!" he exclaimed. "I'll miss you, that's for sure."

Suddenly he reached over and took the cup from my hand. He set it on the wide wooden railing and then, firmly, deliberately, pulled me toward him. His arm was tight around my waist, his face leaned close to mine. . . .

"Hey!" I cried, twisting in his grasp. "Hey, wait a second."

"Wait for what?" Roy asked, not letting go.

"Roy, please, I—"

Roy clicked his tongue. "Aha, sweet sixteen and never been kissed. Come on, you don't have to be shy with me."

I had dreamed about a moment like this, but in my fantasies there was a deep closeness between us, something neither of us had discovered with anyone else before. But now to Roy I was just a date—someone to dance with, to joke with, to kiss.

"Let go of me," I said. "I don't want you to— Just *let go!*"

But Roy didn't seem to take me seriously. Laughing, he held me more tightly than ever. "Relax, will you?" he said indignantly. "I don't bite."

"Hey, what's going on out here?"

Finally Roy let his hands drop to his sides as Bob Hansen loomed in the doorway. He tossed us a sly, knowing look. "Maybe I better come back later, huh?"

"Oh, no, that's okay," I said quickly. "We were just going back in anyway."

Roy frowned, but I guess he decided not to make an issue of it. We trooped back inside just as Stevie was announcing the next number.

"And now for a little change of pace. Here's an oldie for you, an oldie but goody."

"Are you afraid to dance with me, too?" Roy asked as the guitar pealed out the opening chords.

I shook my head. The evening stretched long and bleak ahead of me, and I'd have to get through it somehow. I'd have to keep dancing with him no matter how I felt.

Was Roy mad because I wouldn't let him kiss me, or were his feelings hurt? It was hard to guess how he really felt about anything beneath his teasing, joking veneer. I would never understand him, and he would never understand me.

Slowly we worked our way out to the middle of the dance floor. I caught the words Stevie was singing and smiled wryly: "If you can't be with the one you love, honey, love the one you're with." That was Roy, all right—Roy Lowell all the way.

Suddenly Roy stiffened. For a moment he seemed to lose the beat, and I realized that he was staring past my shoulder at the door. "What's the matter?" I asked. I twisted around to follow his gaze—and saw for myself.

Eilene stood just inside the doorway, her frilly red skirt matching her shining curls. Beside her, his arm linked comfortably through hers as they surveyed the room, stood Brian.

12

The music played on, and Roy and I went right on dancing as if nothing had changed. But as I studied Roy's face, I had the feeling that he was disturbed, bewildered, shaken —just as I was myself.

I'd been feeling such distance between Roy and me that now I couldn't bring myself to speak to him about the thing that was plainly on both our minds. But my feet kept losing the rhythm of the music, and my gaze kept straying across the room to where Brian and Eilene, smiling and at ease, had stepped into the dance.

None of it made any sense. Sure, Brian and his father had done a skit in the *Scandals*, but that was just kind of a lark. What was Brian doing here, at a dance for the summer kids? And why on earth was he here with Eilene?

I remembered so clearly that night as we walked home from the party when Brian told me he thought Eilene was "boring as heck." So what had ever possessed him to invite her tonight?

It just wasn't fair, I thought, and a wave of hurt and anger swept over me. When I had wanted to be with Roy, Eilene was always getting there ahead of me. And now, when Roy just wasn't important anymore, here she was again—with Brian, with my best friend, Brian. It didn't seem right—Brian smiling at her, laughing with her, dancing with her. . . .

"I think they're going to take a break now," Roy said when the song was over. "I want to get something to eat."

It didn't matter to me whether we danced or not. Numbly I followed him to the refreshment table. Liz wasn't there; I glimpsed her out on the dance floor talking to the boy in the red shirt.

I helped myself to a couple of raisin cookies, but I could hardly taste them. Without the music the room seemed suddenly too quiet. Brian and Eilene stood against the far wall, laughing and talking. They hardly glanced over at me and Roy, but they had to be aware of us. They had to know, deep down, what they were doing to me.

Only I didn't quite know myself. I just knew I'd wasted the summer dreaming about Roy, and I knew I should have paid attention to Brian while I had the chance.

Funny, I'd never realized that in quite this way before—not until I saw him with someone else.

Now Carla had joined them. They were too far away for me to hear what they said, but Eilene and Carla seemed to be giggling over something while Brian listened and smiled. It was kind of a patient, tolerant smile, though, as if he were getting bored and restless. He didn't belong over there with them. If we were together, we would whisper and laugh and tell our own private jokes. But I was here with Roy, and Brian was with Eilene—everything was hopelessly mixed up.

"Be back in a minute," Roy muttered. He crossed the room to join Bob Hansen and two other guys who were talking to Stevie. But he kept edging closer to Eilene while he pretended he wasn't watching her every move.

"Hey, are you in charge over here?" asked a long-legged girl in designer jeans. "Looks as though you're running low on punch."

It was true. Only a shallow puddle shimmered at the bottom of the bowl. By now Liz was nowhere in sight. "There's probably more back in the kitchen," I said. "I'll go see."

I was grateful for an excuse to get away by myself. I took my time walking down the long hall to the empty kitchenette. It wasn't much more than an alcove really, with a sink and a refrigerator and a coffee urn donated by the Woman's Club. For a few moments I just leaned against the dusty counter and tried to get my head clear. But I couldn't erase the picture of Eilene and Brian, arm in arm in the doorway.

Finally I opened the refrigerator, and sure enough there was a tall plastic container of fruit punch. As I lifted it from the shelf, I realized I was doing just what Mom or Dad would do at a gathering like this— helping out behind the scenes. And it was fun in a way to know where things were, to make everything run so smoothly no one had to know how the system actually worked. I was glad I could see the party from both sides.

Reluctantly I went back and poured the punch into the big china bowl. I put out some more cookies and made a neat stack of paper napkins. When I looked up, Eilene stood across the table from me, watching me.

"Hi," she said almost in a whisper.

"Hi," I said. And I discovered that I didn't feel angry at her at all. As she wavered there with that timid, half-guilty smile, I had a strange intuition that Eilene and I felt almost the same way. Through some very puzzling set of circumstances we were each here with the wrong person, and we both wanted to set things straight.

"It's a weird party, isn't it?" Eilene said, biting into a cookie.

"I'll say. Things have a way of turning out like you'd never expect."

There was a lot more I could have said, but I felt shy and embarrassed. I couldn't exactly say, "Eilene, let's switch dates. This is a big mess, but maybe we can still salvage something." I didn't dare say, "Please don't be too nice to Brian, don't try to win him over."

"Well," Eilene said. She hesitated, she shifted her weight from one foot to the other as though she wanted to say something else. "See you," was all she said at last, and she drifted away into the crowd.

I stayed there through the whole break, serving up punch and handing out paper plates. Any other time Brian would have been the first to stampede to the refreshment table. But tonight he kept over to the far wall, always with a laughing, chattering crowd. He was avoiding me, there was no doubt about that. And if he had to go hungry to do it, it served him right.

But I couldn't be very mad at Brian, either. If Brian had invited me to the dance, would I have wanted to go with him? Or would I have been disappointed because Roy was the one I'd been dreaming of and scheming after for all these weeks? I'd always just taken Brian for granted, just assumed he'd be there whenever I wanted and needed him. And now maybe it was too late—now I might have lost him.

The only person for me to blame was myself. If I hadn't been so dazzled by Roy, if I had appreciated Brian for the truly special person he was, I might be having a great time right now instead of hiding here behind the refreshment table.

Stevie and the Angels climbed onto the stage again, and Liz returned to the table. "Hey, thanks for taking over," she said. "I really needed a change of scene for a while."

"I'll stay here if you want to go dance," I said, almost pleading with her. Roy was striding toward me, ready to claim me like a piece of luggage.

Liz hesitated, as if she sensed I wasn't simply offering to be polite. "Well, you can hang out here with me if you want," she suggested. "I wouldn't mind company."

I was about to accept when Roy reached us and asked, "You ready? They're going to do a couple of fast ones."

To prove it there was a long drumroll, a squeal from the organ, and the new set began. "Roy," I said, "I'm really not much in a dancing mood."

"What about me?" he demanded. "I'm not exactly thrilled about all this either, you know."

"About all what?" I asked.

"You know what I'm talking about," Roy said, glowering. "Eilene showing up with that guy—what a mess!"

So this was the boy who had tried to kiss

me less than an hour ago. "What difference does that make to you?" I pressed. "Just because Eilene's here with—"

"Oh, forget it, will you?" Roy almost groaned. "I can't explain it. Come on, let's go out there and dance. We'll show them."

Could it be that Roy really did like Eilene, that somehow she meant more to him than he had realized before? Well, he was right about one thing—we'd show them. We'd show Eilene and Brian that we could both have a perfectly good time without them. I'd just be pretending, of course, but at least I might feel better if Brian didn't know how miserable I was.

"Come on, then," I said. "Let's give it a try."

We made our way out onto the dance floor, and somehow I groped for the beat and found it. Numbly at first my hands and feet began to move, but little by little I let my body take over. Roy and I danced a little apart, not touching, but somehow I felt closer to him than I ever had before. Whatever this was, we were in it together.

They approached slowly, as if it was almost by accident. At first Brian's back was to us, but gradually, as he and Eilene danced nearer, he turned to face me. Closer and closer they came, and Brian wore his most mischievous grin—and suddenly he stepped between me and Roy and asked, with the hint of a bow, "Excuse me, may I have this dance, madam?"

I must have blushed to the roots of my hair, but somehow I answered, "Certainly. Thank you."

Brian took both my hands, lightly but firmly, and drew me away to a less crowded part of the floor. I glanced back, and sure enough, they were together, Roy and Eilene. For a moment they were still, just looking at each other. Then Roy said something and they began to dance as if nothing else in the world really mattered.

But I didn't watch them for long. Brian gave my hands a gentle tug. "Well, I've finally got my chance, Marcy," he said. "Now I get to dance with you. Come on."

I'd never even guessed that Brian could dance. I'd always assumed he was the kind of guy who'd rather stay home and read than go to a party. But tonight he was light and sure on his feet, and his grin was so infectious that in a minute or two I forgot all my confusion, forgot to be angry at Roy or Brian or myself, forgot everything except how much fun it was to dance with Brian as my partner.

"Now for a touch of romance." Suddenly Stevie's voice purred over the microphone. "We're going to give you a ballad, something for a very special evening."

Then the song began, low and gentle. Brian's arm slipped around my waist and he pulled me close to him. I remember I had the fleeting thought that it really didn't make any difference that Brian was an inch shorter than I was. It seemed so natural to have his arm around me, to feel the warm pressure of his hand holding mine—so natural, and so right.

We didn't talk much—conversation was always hard anyway above the music. But after three or four numbers Brian said, "Let's go outside a minute," and I knew it couldn't wait any longer. There were just too many things we had to say to each other.

But I didn't know where to begin. We stood a little apart, almost shyly, leaning against the wooden railing. I listened to the muffled throbbing of the music from inside the community house, and watched the big brown moth that still circled the light overhead.

After what felt like a very long time I said, "Boy, you sure surprised me walking in tonight—with Eilene."

"Oh, that." Brian shrugged. "I had to do something, didn't I, to get your attention?"

I looked away. It hurt to admit how right he was. "But why bring Eilene? I thought you didn't—"

"Eilene's not as dumb as she likes people to think," Brian said. "I'll tell you—I met her on the path one day. She didn't know we lived up there, she was just out walking. And she told me the whole story—how she really liked Roy but she got so fed up with him flirting with every girl he saw, she turned him down when he invited her to the dance tonight, and—"

"He invited *her*?" I exclaimed. "When? I thought— When he asked me I thought—"

"Oh, I don't know when exactly. But the thing is, just before he asked her, she caught him walking along the beach holding hands with what's-her-name—that plumpish girl who always looks like she's about to yawn—"

"Carla! He was holding hands with *Carla*?"

Brian grinned. "If you ask me, it shows he hasn't got much taste. Anyway, that was the last straw. Eilene turned him down when he asked her, but she felt awful about it. That's why she was out walking."

"I was only his second choice," I said, and I was laughing. "After all that, I was just second choice—and I don't even care!"

Brian looked like he wasn't sure whether to laugh or not. After a couple of seconds he went on. "So I ran into Eilene and she was so upset she actually started telling me the whole story. *Me,* when she hardly even knew me. And I knew by then you were going with Roy, so somehow Eilene and I just decided we'd go together. That's all."

"Then you really didn't go with her like a regular date?" I cried, swept with relief. "You just went with her to make her feel better, right?"

"Well, not just that," Brian said, and a

knot tightened somewhere in my chest. "There was a lot more to it than that."

Eilene's not as dumb as she likes people to think, he had said. If he hadn't asked her to the dance out of sympathy, then did that mean he had changed his mind about her, had begun to care for her. . . .

"I knew I'd been moping around too much," Brian said. "If I wanted you to be interested in me, I had to be interesting, right? That's how I ended up doing the skit in the *Scandals,* kind of trying to impress you, I suppose. And I was all set to ask you to that dance the night we went for ice cream, too. It just seems like all summer I've been missing my chances, coming in too late. . . ."

"Too late?" I repeated. "What do you mean?"

"Oh, I mean—I'm trying to say . . ." But words failed him. He gave up trying to use them, reached out, and drew me into his arms.

Maybe someday I would tell him how Roy tried to kiss me an hour before under the same porch light with the same fluttering moth. But in that moment Brian's kiss erased everything that had ever happened before and swept away all thought about things to come. Only the two of us existed, just me and Brian floating in a velvet bubble.

I laughed as we stepped apart at last. "You mean that's why? Really?"

"Really," Brian said. "Cross my heart."

"But why didn't you say something?" I cried. "If you wanted to ask me to the dance, why didn't you?"

"Is it true or is it not true that you were thinking about Roy all summer?" he asked quietly.

I looked away, ashamed and sorry. "You know," I said, "I always thought you were the one who hates to admit when you're wrong. But that's what I've been doing all summer. I should have listened to you. You can't really get hung up on somebody like Roy. He doesn't want to be serious about anything, or anybody."

Our hands locked together on the wide wooden railing. "I did want to warn you," Brian said. "I didn't want to see you getting hurt. But mostly, I've got to admit, I was just being selfish."

"The first minute I saw Roy something told me he was just the kind of guy who expected girls to worship him," I said. "But I just put that out of my mind, along with everything else. And then all of a sudden tonight everything became clear. It's as though I'd been running as fast as I could in the wrong direction and finally you got me to turn around."

It was all right. I felt it in the squeeze of his hand. "Do you think your escort will object if I steal you for the rest of the evening?" Brian asked. "Not that it much matters. I'm going to, whether he likes it or not."

"I think," I said, giggling, "he and Eilene won't even notice."

"Well, then, let's go," Brian said. "They're having a big dance in there—let's not miss any more of it."

13

The Murphys' cottage was deserted. One by one I cranked the jalousies shut and rolled down the bamboo shades until the front porch was as dark and stifling as a closet.

Mom appeared in the living-room doorway, broom in hand. She dropped a lone rubber flipper into the cardboard box we were filling with what Brian called "flotsam and jetsam." "From under the bed," she said. "You haven't come across the other one, have you?"

I shook my head and pointed to my own pile of treasures: some plastic cowboys and Indians, a harmonica, a red sneaker well-gnawed by Tania the cocker spaniel.

Mom sighed. "Wouldn't you think they could at least close the windows before they left? Honestly, some people are so help-less."

"I guess they had all they could handle just rounding up the twins," I said. "You can't expect too much beyond that."

"I suppose that's true," Mom said. "Be-sides, they know we're here to pick up after them."

I had to smile to myself as I fastened down the last shade. It had been a summer unique in the history of Lake Marinac, but certain things would never change.

Outside, there was a rumble of wheels and I opened the front door to see Dad and Brian as they rolled the Murphys' alumi-num outboard on a dolly toward the garage. Brian had dropped by that morning as we were clearing up after breakfast and of-fered his help. After all, it was Labor Day, he pointed out. Around here that meant a day of labor for us.

Mom and I joined them outside. It was a gray, overcast day, too cold for swimming. "Well," Dad said, mopping his forehead with his sleeve, "we'll get that awning down and that'll do it for the Murphys. Who've we got next?"

"Lowells, I guess," said Mom. "You know, the MacDonald place."

Not long ago I would have tensed inside at the very mention of the name. And I would have ached with a secret grief know-ing that today Roy had gone, without even saying good-bye to me, for a whole long winter.

But now I just glanced over at Brian and we exchanged a knowing smile. I knew Brian would like nothing better than to sweep away the last traces of Roy Lowell along with the dust and the flotsam and jetsam.

"Marcy, let's you and me go up there and make sure they're gone," Brian suggested. "I think they weren't leaving till late."

"You really can't wait, can you?" I giggled as we started up Lakefront Road.

"Oh, I wouldn't say that." Brian grinned. "Actually I'll kind of miss Mrs. Lowell. You've got to admit there's a certain flair about her. And she was neat to work with in the *Scandals*."

"Hey, how are Tom and Kate getting along?" I asked.

"Like milk and lemon juice," Brian grunted. "It's a disaster. Tom hitched down to the city to see her and she was out on a date when he got there. So all the money he figured he'd use to take her out he spent on bus fare home."

We both laughed. No one had to say it— Kate and Roy had a lot in common.

We rounded the bend in the road and there in the drive stood the Lowells' blue station wagon. Boxes and suitcases were piled high in the back, and two sets of water skis were strapped to the roof. The door on the passenger's side gaped open, and leaning against it, their arms wrapped around each other, stood Roy and Eilene.

Roy must have heard our steps on the gravel. For an instant he looked up and his mouth opened as if he were about to call a greeting. Then he seemed to remember himself; he remembered, perhaps, that, after all, this was a special moment of parting. Without a word he bent toward Eilene again as Brian and I turned and stole away.

"I thought he was going to call to me," I said when we were out of earshot. "I was kind of glad he didn't."

"I think he really does like Eilene," Brian mused. "Maybe his thing about flirting with every girl is kind of a bad habit he's trying to break."

"He'll have to," I said, "or he'll lose her." And in my mind I added, the way he did me.

Mom and Dad had the awning down by the time we got back. "They're not gone yet," I explained. "You better give them a while."

"Anything else we can do to help?" Brian asked.

If only we could have some time to ourselves, I thought. There were only two days left before school began, with its rigid routine that devoured our freedom. I longed to make up for some of the time I had wasted this summer, time I could have been sharing with Brian.

Dad surveyed the Murphys' house and

yard, searching for an assignment. Everything was in order, but his gaze strayed to the Spaldings' cottage down the road. There were flowerpots to take in, shutters to fasten, probably even the remains of last night's farewell party to clear away. I might as well accept it, there was enough work to keep us busy till ten o'clock tonight.

It was Mom who came to the rescue. "You kids have worked all afternoon," she said. "Let's all take a break—it'll keep till tomorrow."

"Thanks," Brian and I said in unison. We laughed and he added, "We'll go for a walk —maybe we'll pick some blackberries."

But as we started along the beach, I turned to him and reminded him, "Hey, we forgot to bring a pail."

Brian made an exaggerated double take. "Oh, no! Then we'll have to use my hat!" He reached up to pat his hair and brought back an empty hand. "My hat! I forgot my hat too! What will we do?" But by then we were both shaking with laughter and we forgot all about blackberries.

We crossed the beach and started along the path toward Brian's house. But a few yards in, he stopped and pointed up the overgrown trail that led off to the right, away from the lake. "Want to climb up there?" he asked.

"Sure, to the lookout?"

"Why not? We can make it."

We turned from the path and started single file up the trail, stepping carefully among tumbled rocks and fallen logs. Brian walked ahead, holding leafy branches aside for me as we wound our way upward. Once I stopped to free the leg of my jeans from a clutching briar, and once Brian held up his hand and we both froze to hear the clear questioning whistle of a bobwhite only a stone's throw off the trail.

And I knew that there was nowhere else I would rather be than climbing up to the lookout, just Brian and I alone together.

In half an hour we broke through the last tangle of thorns and underbrush and emerged on a bald dome of rock that crowned the hill. For a few moments we just stood in silence gazing down at the lake, which glistened smooth and still. I could make out the cove where the Townsends' canoe would still be lying belly up on the sand. And off to the left, around a bend in the shore, the roofs of cottages lay in a neat geometric pattern. The summer village, abandoned now until another season.

"If you could be some kind of weather," Brian said suddenly, "what would you want to be?"

It had been so long since we played the impressions game! I thought a minute. "I think a wind, whistling down over the hills and making waves on the lake," I said. "And grabbing people's hats."

"I think I'd be the sun just breaking through the clouds," Brian said. "Like up there—look."

And it was true. For the first time that day the sun peeked down at us through the gray blanket of clouds overhead.

Brian sat down on a jutting boulder and I crouched beside him on a mossy rock. "It's been a pretty incredible summer," he said.

"It sure has," I said. "When I think how funny I always used to feel around those summer kids, and now I can talk to them and hang around with them if I want, and play duets with Liz—I feel like a different person."

"Me too," Brian said. He reached down and touched my hair. "Maybe it's a good thing Roy Lowell turned up this summer— that's what it took for me to finally figure out how I really felt about you."

"I don't know why it took me so long, but I finally caught up with you," I said. "When you walked in with Eilene the other night, I finally figured out how I felt about you, too."

"Well, that was the general idea." Brian's hands rested on my shoulders and he rose, gently lifting me to my feet. "I hope you're glad I thought of it."

"Very glad," I whispered, as he drew me to him and pressed his lips to mine.

I don't know how long we stood there together—until a wind sprung up and Brian said, "Hey, you're shivering. Maybe we better start back down."

"I hate to go," I told him. "It's so nice here—I hate to let go of this moment."

"But nothing is ending," Brian said softly. "This is just the beginning."

"That's a promise?"

"Cross my heart."

This time I went first, laughing and skidding down the long twisting trail. As we neared the bottom, I broke into a run. Brian didn't catch up with me until we reached the shore of the lake.

If you enjoyed this book...

...you will enjoy a *First Love* from Silhouette subscription even more. It will bring you each new title, as soon as it is published every month, delivered right to your door.

Filled with the challenges, excitement and anticipation that make first love oh, so wonderful, *First Love* romances are new and different. Every *First Love* romance is an original novel—never before published—and all written by leading authors.

If you enjoyed this book, treat yourself, or some friend, to a one-year subscription to these romantic originals. We'll ship two NEW $1.75 romances each month, a total of 24 books a year. So send in your coupon now. **There's nothing quite as special as a First Love.**

First Love from Silhouette

THERE'S NOTHING QUITE AS SPECIAL AS A FIRST LOVE.

$1.75 each

1 ☐ NEW BOY IN TOWN
Dorothy Francis

2 ☐ GIRL IN THE ROUGH
Josephine Wunsch

3 ☐ PLEASE LET ME IN
Patti Beckman

4 ☐ SERENADE
Adrienne Marceau

5 ☐ FLOWERS FOR LISA
Veronica Ladd

6 ☐ KATE HERSELF
Helen Erskine

7 ☐ SONGBIRD
Carrie Enfield

8 ☐ SPECIAL GIRL
Dorothy Francis

9 ☐ LOVE AT FIRST SIGHT
Elaine Harper

10 ☐ PLEASE LOVE ME ... SOMEBODY
Maud Johnson

11 ☐ IT'S MY TURN
Eleni Carr

12 ☐ IN MY SISTER'S SHADOW
Genell Dellin

13 ☐ SOMETIME MY LOVE
Oneta Ryan

14 ☐ PROMISED KISS
Veronica Ladd

15 ☐ SUMMER ROMANCE
Rebecca Diamond

16 ☐ SOMEONE TO LOVE
Ann Bryan

17 ☐ GOLDEN GIRL
Helen Erskine

18 ☐ WE BELONG TOGETHER
Elaine Harper

19 ☐ TOMORROW'S WISH
Oneta Ryan

20 ☐ SAY PLEASE!
Dorothy Francis

21 ☐ TEACH ME TO LOVE
Wendi Davis

22 ☐ THAT SPECIAL SUMMER
Deborah Kent

FIRST LOVE, Department FL/4
1230 Avenue of the Americas
New York, NY 10020

Please send me the books I have checked above. I am enclosing $_____ (please add 50¢ to cover postage and handling. NYS and NYC residents please add appropriate sales tax). Send check or money order—no cash or C.O.D.'s please. Allow six weeks for delivery.

NAME_____

ADDRESS_____

CITY_____ STATE/ZIP_____

6 brand new Silhouette Romance novels yours for 15 days—Free!

If you enjoyed this Silhouette First Love, and would like to move on to even more thrilling, satisfying stories then Silhouette Romances are for you. Enjoy the challenges, conflicts, and joys of love. Sensitive heroines will enchant you—powerful heroes will delight you as they sweep you off to adventures around the world.

6 Silhouette Romances, free for 15 days!

We'll send you 6 new Silhouette Romances to keep for 15 days, absolutely free! If you decide not to keep them, send them back to us. You pay nothing.

FREE HOME DELIVERY. But if you enjoy them as much as we think you will, keep them by paying the invoice enclosed with your free trial shipment. You'll then automatically become a member of the Silhouette Book Club and receive 6 more new Silhouette romances every month.

There is no minimum number of books to buy and you can cancel at any time.

Imagine . . . you on the cover of a First Love Romance!

Announcing the
First Love from Silhouette cover girl contest.^{SM}

Now's your chance to see your face on thousands of First Love from Silhouette romances all over the country!

It's like a dream come true—but it could happen, if you win the First Love from Silhouette cover girl contest.^{SM}

Just send in a recent photo of yourself, along with a completed entry blank (below), to *Tiger Beat* magazine. Contest open to nonprofessionals only. Look for complete details in the June and July issues of *Tiger Beat* and *Tiger Beat Star.*

Four finalists will be flown free to Hollywood for judging on August 20 and 21. The lucky winner will also win a model fee of $250, and a trip to New York for a photography session. (Parent of guardian may accompany if winner is under 18.) Date of session will be determined according to winner's availability. Entries must be postmarked no later than June 30, 1982, so enter now!

READERS' COMMENTS ON FIRST LOVE BOOKS

"I am very pleased with the First Love Books by Silhouette. Thank you for making a book that I can enjoy."

—G.O.*, Indianapolis, IN

"I just want you to know that I love the Silhouette First Love Books. They put me in a happy mood. Please don't stop selling them!"

—M.H.*, Victorville, CA

"I loved the First Love book that I read. It was great! I loved every single page of it. I plan to read many more of them."

—R.B.*, Picayune, MS

* names available upon request

Dear Reader:

Please take a few moments to fill out this questionnaire. It will help us give you more of the First Love books you'd like best.

Mail to: **Karen Solem**
Silhouette Books
1230 Ave. of the Americas, New York, N.Y. 10020

1. Where did you obtain **THAT SPECIAL SUMMER?**

10-1 ☐ **Bookstore**   -6 ☐ **Newsstand**
-2 ☒ **Supermarket**   -7 ☐ **Friend**
-3 ☐ **Variety/discount store**   -8 ☐ **Other:** _____
-4 ☐ **Department store**   (write in)
-5 ☐ **Drug store**

2. How many FIRST LOVE books have you read including this one? (circle one number) 11- 1 2 3 4 5 6 7 8 9 or (more)

3. Overall, how would you rate this book?
12-1 ☒ **Excellent**   -2 ☐ **Very good**
-3 ☐ **Good**   -4 ☐ **Fair**   -5 ☐ **Poor**

4. Which elements did you like **best** about this book?
13-1 ☐ **Heroine** -2 ☐ **Hero** -3 ☐ **Other characters**
-4 ☒ **Love scenes** -5 ☒ **Setting** -6 ☐ **Story line** -7 ☐ **Ending**

5. Which elements did you like **least** about this book?
14-1 ☐ **Heroine** -2 ☐ **Hero** -3 ☒ **Other characters**
-4 ☐ **Love scenes** -5 ☐ **Setting** -6 ☐ **Story line** -7 ☐ **Ending**

6. What influenced you to buy this book?
15-1 ☐ **Cover** -2 ☐ **Title** -3 ☒ **Back cover description**
-4 ☐ **Recommendations** -5 ☒ **You buy other FIRST LOVE books**

7. How many new FIRST LOVE books would you be interested in buying each month? (circle one number) 16- 1 2 3 4 5 or (more)

8. Please check the box next to your age group.
17-1 ☐ **Under 12**   -3 ☐ **15-16**   -5 ☐ **19-20**   -7 ☐ **24-35**
-2 ☒ **12-14**   -4 ☐ **17-18**   -6 ☐ **21-23**   -8 ☐ **35 and older**

Name _Kathy Lolos_
Address _134 Easy St._
City _Wenatchee_ State _Wash._ Zip _98801_

18 ___ 19 82 20 ___ 21 ___ 22 ___